IN BETWEEN WORLDS

By
Abner Al-Ameen

In Between Worlds

ACKNOWLEDGEMENTS

First, I would like to acknowledge my wife Angela, whom I live my life to impress.

I would like to acknowledge my mother: (born) Myrtle A. Moore – my real-life super-hero.

I would also like to acknowledge Ryan Coogler and Aaron McGruder – my industry heroes.

I would like to acknowledge all of my family, friends, and fans of fantasy fiction for overwhelming me with love. This book is dedicated to you.

And thank you Atlanta for your support.

There is no place like home.

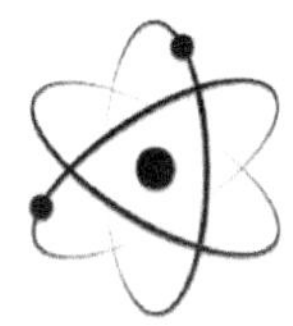

IN
BETWEEN
WORLDS

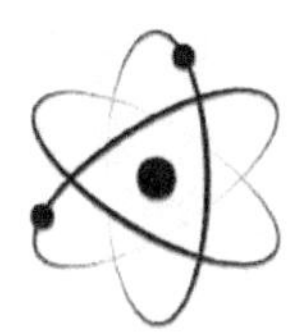

PROLOGUE

Elian dreamed of running through his house. He could feel the carpet beneath his feet, but the floor felt strange tonight – soft, almost liquid. When he tried to stop, his toes sank in. He pitched forward, shoulders first, and passed through the wall, as though the plaster had turned to water. It wasn't like falling. It was worse. He felt the wooden studs slide through his chest, saw the paint blister across his vision, smelled the chalky grit of drywall in his mouth. And then he was back.

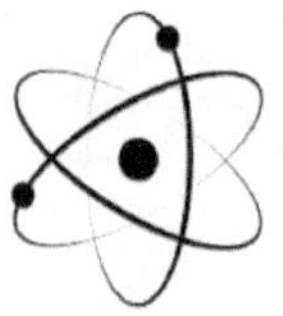

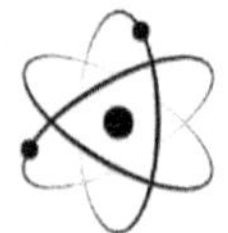

CHAPTER 1

The Fracture

The drywall screamed before Elian did.

It cracked in a jagged line above his bed, the plaster trembling like chattering teeth in the cold. His arm was already inside the wall up to the elbow when the first sound left his throat.

"Mom!"

Janelle Freeman woke instantly, her body already moving before her mind caught up. She stumbled down the hall, bare feet smacking against the wood, heart pounding in her ears. Marcus was right behind her, his big frame blotting out the nightlight's glow.

The sight in Elian's room stopped her cold.

Her son's right arm had vanished into the wall beside his

bed. Not pressed. Not broken. Not crushed. Gone, as if the house had decided to swallow him whole. His small chest heaved, each scream making the plaster bulge unnaturally around the outline of his ribs.

"God, no," Janelle whispered, her voice splitting. She ran to him, clutching at his wrist, but the wall clutched tighter, refusing to let go.

"Don't pull!" Marcus yelled, though his own hands were already digging, clawing at painted plaster like a man trying to dig through stone with his bare fingers. "Janelle – call!"

She was already fumbling for the phone, shaking so hard she almost dialed wrong. "My son – my son's stuck in the wall!"

The dispatcher's calm voice was swallowed by the chaos. Elian's eyes rolled back, sweat soaking his hairline. His body jerked, half in this world, half not.

Marcus pressed his forehead against the wall, his voice breaking into a hoarse whisper meant for only one listener. "Hold on, son. I'm here. Don't you let go, you hear me? You hold on."

The sirens came too slow.

By the time paramedics burst in – saws whining, masks snapping into place – Elian had stopped screaming. He whimpered as they carved a jagged square of drywall around his small body, cutting the house away from him piece by piece.

When they lifted him onto the gurney, sheet rock dust still clinging to his lashes, Janelle's knees buckled.

Marcus caught her before she hit the floor, though his own face was gray, hollow. He'd thought he'd known fear before – the day his mother died, the night Janelle miscarried – but this was different. This was fear that the world itself might decide to erase their boy.

As the ambulance doors slammed shut, Janelle whispered through her tears: "Why does this keep happening?"

Marcus had no answer. The wail of sirens filled the silence for him.

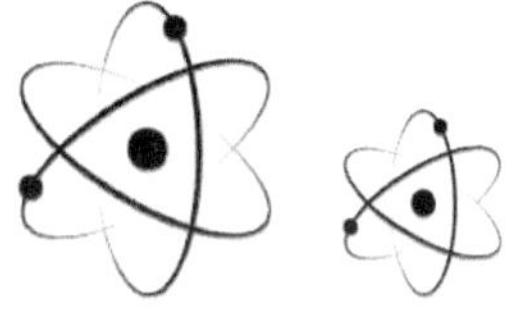

CHAPTER 2

Grady Hospital

The emergency room stank of antiseptic and burnt coffee. The fluorescent lights buzzed like trapped yellow jackets.

Nurses rolled Elian into radiology while Marcus argued at the desk, demanding answers.

"He was inside the wall!" Marcus's voice carried too loud, too desperate. "Half his chest was in there – look at him!"

Doctors whispered behind clipboards. The CT scan blurred, bone structures unreadable, as if the machine itself refused to see him.

Elian lay curled on the gurney, IV in his arm, eyelids heavy.

Janelle smoothed his hair with trembling fingers. "Baby," she whispered, "tell them what you told us."

His lips moved. "I...fall through things when I sleep."

The attending physician frowned, jotting down a note. "Night terrors," she muttered. "Possible seizures, confusion, we'll schedule neurology –"

"He wasn't dreaming," Marcus snapped. His hands shook as he pointed to the bruises and cuts on Elian's shoulder where the wood had sheared his skin.

Before the physician could respond, nurses wheeled in machines, checked monitors, and whispered words Janelle couldn't catch. Janelle's lips moved silently, but her prayers felt hollow.

Marcus turned to a young surgeon, fury spilling over.

"You don't understand," Marcus said, voice rising, drawing stares. "This isn't some – some accident. This is the fourth time. Fourth! And you people keep cutting him open like he's a damn science experiment."

The young surgeon, overburdened by exhaustion more than authority, lifted his head defensively. "Mr. Freeman, with respect, your son presents a tissue trauma we've never seen before. Every time he...what did you call it, phases? His cells are forced through solid matter. That's catastrophic. If we don't operate..."

"Operate on what?" Marcus barked. "You don't even know what's happening."

Janelle flinched. He wasn't wrong, but the fury in his voice cut sharper than any scalpel.

Dr. Henry entered then, brisk and business-like, his badge

swinging as he walked. He was in his late 40s, hair graying at the temples; his whole presence reeked of suspicion. He gave Janelle a tight nod before turning his attention to Marcus.

"Mr. Freeman," Henry said. "I've reviewed your son's file. Dozens of hospital visits. Multiple exploratory surgeries. And yet – you've declined psychiatric evaluation."

Marcus stiffened. "Because he's not crazy."

"No one is suggesting he is," Henry said evenly, though his eyes said otherwise. "But children don't just...fuse into walls. Sometimes, the mind creates the body's illness. Sometimes, trauma manifests in..."

"Don't you dare," Janelle cut in, her voice louder than expected. "Don't you dare put this on my son's mind. He's eleven. He's..."

Her throat closed. "He's just a boy."

Henry softened his tone, but not his stare. "Mrs. Freeman, sometimes the subconscious is more powerful than we realize. I only want answers as much as you do."

No one had answers.

None but one.

CHAPTER 3

Somewhere over the Atlantic

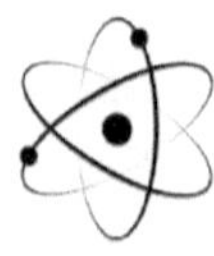

Xinavane stared out of the window into the vast black sky. The darkness outside was thick and endless, the Atlantic Ocean far below. The engines rumbled beneath her seat — not loud, but constant.

She hadn't slept. Not in hours. Maybe not really at all.

The plane had lifted from Johannesburg just after midnight. Now she sat between worlds, neither here nor there. She closed her eyes. She told herself she was only resting.

Instead, she slipped.

The dream came fast, uncoiling like a snake.

She stood barefoot in a field that stretched endlessly. The ground pulsed beneath her feet, like the beat of a giant heart.

Voices drifted at the edge of hearing – too remote to grasp – until one rose clear.

"Elian."

The name hung in the air like fog.

Her breath caught. She turned toward the sound and saw a child in the distance – thin shoulders, trembling hands pressed against a wall that wasn't there. His face remained a shadow, but his eyes...his eyes were wide with terror.

"Stay with me," she whispered, though she didn't know why.

The boy looked up, and the ground split beneath them both.

Xinavane jerked awake, heart hammering, the dream still clinging to her skin. The cabin lights glowed dim blue; passengers slept around her, mouths open, bodies slack. The turbulence eased, but the pressure in her chest did not.

She leaned back and closed her eyes again.

But she did not sleep.

In her mind, the name echoed heavier each time.

"Elian."

She whispered it once, testing it against her tongue, as though saying it aloud might summon him closer...or warn her that he was already near.

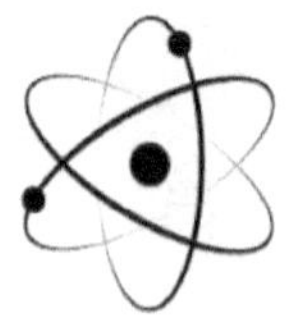

CHAPTER 4

Internal Conflict 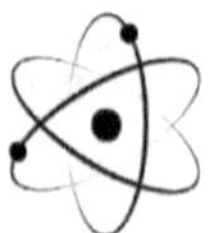

The doors to the trauma bay hissed open, and a nurse stepped out, mask hanging loose at her throat.

"He's stable," she said. "Sedated for now. You can sit with him."

Janelle didn't wait. She rushed past, her breath breaking as she took her son's hand. Elian's face was damp, lips dry, eyelids fluttering. He murmured something under sedation, words slurred but distinct.

Not English.

The syllables spilled from his mouth in a language she didn't know, harsh and rolling, like distant thunder.

Janelle froze. Her hand trembling against his. "Marcus," she whispered. "He's speaking."

Marcus leaned close, brow furrowed. "What is that? French? No – no, I don't –"

Dr. Henry moved close too, frowning as though cataloging every sound.

And then, Elian's body shuddered. Not violently, yet suddenly. A ripple beneath his skin, as if he wasn't entirely anchored to the bed.

The monitor beeped. The air thickened.

For one awful second, Janelle swore she could see the sheet beneath him through the outline of his arm.

"God," she breathed, clutching him tighter, as if her grip alone could hold him here.

Henry's jaw tightened. "That was psychosomatic."

Marcus let out a short, humorless laugh. "You think?"

But Janelle barely heard them. She leaned close to her son's ear, whispering in desperation the same words she'd whispered since the night they'd brought him home from the adoption agency:

"I love you so much. I will never leave you."

CHAPTER 5

Xinavane Arrives

Dr. Henry had retreated into some office, leaving Janelle and Marcus adrift in silence, their boy sedated beyond the glass wall.

When the doors hissed open, Janelle barely looked up – another doctor, another clipboard.

But the woman who entered didn't move like hospital staff.

She came in quietly, as though she had always been in the room. Every step calculated, unhurried. She wore no white coat. Carried no clipboard. No badge. Only a tailored charcoal dress, a handwritten name tag, and a stillness that made the room feel smaller.

Dr. Xinavane was tall, her skin-deep brown, her salt-and-pepper hair drawn into a knot at the nape of her neck. Her eyes seemed older than her face.

"Mr. and Mrs. Freeman?" Her accent carried the weight of Johannesburg. Her voice was smooth, rounded, mixed with something Janelle couldn't place.

Marcus straightened, suspicion heightened. "Who the hell are you?"

"Someone who believes him," Xinavane said simply.

Janelle stumbled over her name. "zen-ah…Vain?"

"shee-nah-Vah-neh." Xinavane corrected her gently, the rhythm shifting, syllables in Tsonga sliding beneath English.

"May I see him?" Xinavane asked.

Janelle answered defensively, "We've had every kind of doctor already. Neurologists, radiologists, surgeons. None of them can tell us anything."

"I'm not here for charts or scans," Xinavane said. Her voice remained calm – but carried a gravity that made Marcus hesitate. "I only need to see him."

Something in the way she said it – not a plea, not an argument, but inevitability – made Janelle nod despite herself.

Inside the observation room, Elian lay pale beneath monitors, his chest rising shallowly. The drywall dust gone now, scrubbed away by nurses, but Xinavane could feel it – the residue, the fracture beneath the skin.

She drew closer, ignoring the skeptical murmur of a nearby resident. She bent until her face was level with Elian's and listened.

The boy's lip moved. His voice was faint, cracked by sedation, but the words were unmistakable. Harsh consonants, rolling vowels, the rhythm of a language neither parent recognized.

Janelle's hand gripped her husband's tight. "He's been doing that. Talking in tongues."

"It's…Xhosa," Xinavane said, listening not only to the words, but what lay beneath them.

Then it happened – so quickly, Marcus almost missed it.

Elian's arm vibrated, flesh rippling, resisting its own boundaries. The sheets beneath him flickered into view through his wrist – then vanished.

Marcus cursed and stepped back. Janelle clapped a hand over her mouth.

Xinavane didn't flinch.

Her gaze sharpened. Her breath stayed steady.

"He's not broken," she said quietly. "He is…in between."

She turned to face them fully, the weight of her presence filling the room.

"If you will allow me, I can reach him."

For the first time since the night began, Marcus's voice carried hope instead of rage. "You can help him?"

Xinavane's eyes softened – though the shadows beneath

them did not. "I can try. But you must understand – this is not an illness. It's a passage."

Janelle looked from Xinavane to her son, torn between fear and hopelessness.

As if in response, Elian shuddered again. His eyelids flickered, as though somewhere deep inside, he recognized her already.

"There are things you need to understand," Xinavane continued, voice low, edged with gravity. "This…what is happening to Elian – is not unique. Not here. And not just with him."

Janelle's eyes widened. "What do you mean?"

Xinavane exhaled, slow and steady. "When I was a child in Johannesburg, I was like him. I phased uncontrollably. I didn't understand it. My parents feared for me, and so did the people who monitored the unusual."

Marcus leaned forward, tense. "Monitored? Like government?"

Xinavane shook her head. "No, worse. Private interests. People who claim to protect, but really…they exploited."

She paused, letting the words settle.

"I've worked with other children long before you ever heard of Elian," she continued.

"There was a girl in Limpopo – opened her mouth and three voices spoke at once. A boy in Soweto – disappeared into the floor and could only be retrieved with precise guidance. My own sister...she screamed for three days, even after her body gave out."

Janelle felt a chill move through her. "So...this isn't just about our son?"

"No," Xinavane said. "It's about all of them. Children like Elian. Gifts they cannot control at first, but which attract attention. Attention from people who will stop at nothing to regulate, contain, or worse."

Silence filled the room.

Somewhere beyond the glass, a monitor beeped steadily.

CHAPTER 6

Into the Subconscious

The room they gave her was small, windowless, and painted an oppressive shade of beige.

A reclining chair sat in the center, its vinyl cracked from years of use. Beside it, a rolling tray held a half-working lamp. The noise of the hospital beyond was muffled, but persistent – the rattle of gurneys, the distant bark of the intercom, the relentless beep of machines.

Elian, awake now, perched himself on the chair like it might bite him. His thin arms wrapped his torso. He wouldn't look at Xinavane.

Marcus crouched down beside him, forcing a smile. "She's here to help, son. Just...talk to her, that's all."

Elian's voice came out small. "She's not a real doctor."

"I was," Xinavane said gently, settling into the chair across from him. "A surgeon, once. But now I work with...dreams."

That made him glance at her – quick, wary. His eyes were rimmed with exhaustion, shadows too heavy for eleven years.

Janelle stood near the door, arms folded tight, fists clenched. She didn't trust this woman – this stranger with her strange calmness. But something in Marcus's face – the way hope had softened him – kept her silent.

Xinavane leaned forward, elbows on her knees, her tone low and even. "Elian, when you sleep, do you ever feel like the world...doesn't stay put?"

He stared at the floor.

"It shifts," she continued, her voice rhythmic, almost musical. "Walls breathe. Floors melt. Your body floats. Sometimes it gets stuck, sometimes it slips through, yes?"

His arms tightened. "I don't like it."

"No. Of course not," Xinavane said reassuringly. "But I can teach you to visit those places without fear. How to walk through them – instead of falling."

For a moment, his eyes widened – curiosity, perhaps. Then he shook his head hard. "No. When I close my eyes, bad things happen."

He slid off the chair, pressing himself against the wall as if to anchor his body to something solid.

Marcus reached for him. "Elian –"

Xinavane lifted a hand, stopping him. Her gaze never left the boy. "You are stronger than you think," she said. "But you must let me in. If you slam the door, the dreams will only knock harder."

Elian's breathing quickened. "I don't want you in my head!"

The monitor spiked.

The wall behind him trembled. Its surface blurred – beginning to fade like a trick of light.

Janelle gasped.

Marcus lunged forward, pulling Elian back just as the wall threatened to swallow him.

The boy trembled in his father's arms, eyes wild. "Don't let her do it, Dad. Don't let her do it!"

The room fell into silence, except for Elian's ragged breathing.

Xinavane exhaled slowly, folding her hands in her lap. Her expression gave nothing away.

"This is only the beginning," she said quietly, almost to herself.

Janelle's eyes burned into her. "You see what you're doing to him?"

Xinavane met her gaze calmly, though her voice was edged with steel now. "No, what he is doing is leaking through. His body does not always stay bound to this world," she bit back. "I'm not the danger here, Mrs. Freeman. The danger is leaving him alone with it."

No one spoke.

Marcus looked between them, torn, holding his son as if he might dissolve at any second.

Elian, eyes squeezed shut against his father's chest, whispered again – words that didn't belong to any language they knew. The syllables slithered into the room like smoke.

Xinavane tilted her head, listening. A hint of recognition crossed her face.

Then she murmured, almost reverently:

"He's already halfway through."

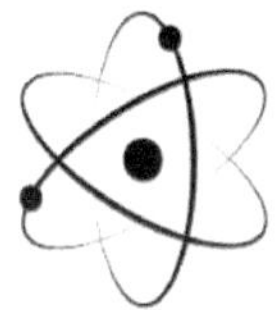

CHAPTER 7

Fault Lines

Janelle stood at the kitchen sink long after the dishes were done, hands braced against the counter, staring at nothing.

Behind her, Marcus dropped into a chair at the table, the wood groaning beneath his weight. He dragged both hands down his face, the exhaustion in him deeper than the circles under his eyes.

"She's not staying," Janelle said without turning.

Marcus let his hands fall. "Janelle —"

"No." Her voice was tight. "Whatever she's doing — whatever that was today — did you see our son? He was terrified. He's a child, Marcus. He doesn't need...trances. He needs safety."

Marcus stared at the scarred tabletop, the grain worn down

by years of meals and laughter that suddenly felt like someone else's life.

"He's not safe." He said quietly. "You saw the wall. You've
seen the hospital bills. Every time it happens, he gets
weaker. He can't keep going like this."

"He needs doctors," Janelle snapped. "Real doctors...not –"
her voice breaking – "not some woman with a pretty accent
and stories about dreams."

Marcus's jaw tightened. "That *'woman'* is the first person
who didn't look at him like a freak."

Janelle spun around, eyes flashing. "And what if she makes
it worse, huh? What if she opens some door he can't close?
I won't let her turn him into an experiment."

The word hung heavy between them.

Experiment.

They both remembered the way doctors lingered too long
at Elian's bedside, how research notes piled higher than
treatment plans. Janelle had sworn to protect him from that
– protect him from being reduced to a case file instead of a
boy.

Marcus leaned back, his expression raw. "We adopted him
to give him a home. Not a prison."

The words struck deep.

Every locked window. Every night she sat outside his door
to keep watch. Every whispered prayer that he would stay

in his bed. Even the decision to homeschool him.

A cage.

Janelle pressed her fist to her mouth, blinking back tears. "If she hurts him…"

Marcus stood and moved beside her. His hand settled on her shoulder – heavy, warm. "Then we stop her. But if she's right – if she can help him – don't we have to try?"

Janelle turned away, staring out the darkened window. The neighborhood was still alive: the streetlamps began to illuminate the manicured lawns, children being called inside, the ordinary world continuing without them.

But she couldn't shake the feeling that eyes were on the house.

That something had followed them home from the hospital.

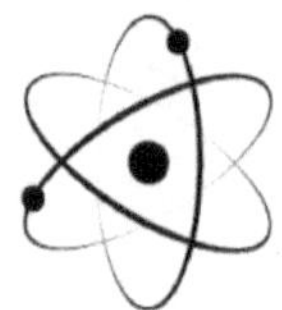 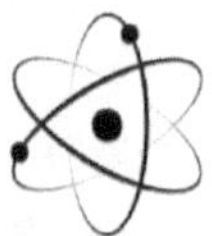

CHAPTER 8

Shadows at the Door

The mailbox rattled in the wind, though the night was still.

Inside, Janelle leaned against the kitchen counter, stirring tea she hadn't the appetite to drink. Marcus could sense Janelle's uneasiness and had checked the front windows for the third time in ten minutes.

Elian lay in his bed upstairs, finally asleep.

And then – there was a knock.

Marcus froze. It was too late for visitors. Too quiet for mistakes.

Janelle's grip tightened on the mug. "Who is it?"

Marcus crept to the door, peering through the peephole. Outside, a man in a dark suit stood under the porch light. His posture was perfect, professional. But there was something about his stillness, the absence of any impatience, that made Marcus's stomach tighten.

He opened the door just a crack.

"Mr. and Mrs. Freeman?" The man's voice was smooth, measured. He held an unmarked folder at his side. "My name is Agent Douglas. We're here regarding your son's condition.

Janelle's hands flew to her chest. "*Condition?*"

"Yes," Douglas said casually, as if discussing a scheduling matter. "We have reason to believe Elian possesses abilities that could have...unforeseen consequences. For his safety and yours, we are authorized to discuss options for temporary relocation."

Marcus's jaw clenched. "*Relocation?* My son is staying right here."

Douglas's eyes slipped past Marcus toward the darkened staircase.

"We understand your concern. But this is serious. Children like him – children with gifts – are...well, they are rare. And they attract attention."

Janelle shook her head, backing away. "No. We're not sending him anywhere. And we don't want anyone interfering with his care."

Douglas's expression didn't change. "Then please consider this an official advisory. We will be monitoring the situation. For his safety."

Before Marcus could respond, the man handed them a small envelope, white and unmarked, then turned and walked to the SUV parked just past the curb. The engine purred, the lights dimmed, and the vehicle rolled into the shadows.

Janelle closed the door and leaned against it, her hands shaking. "What...what does that mean?"

Marcus opened the envelope, eyes scanning the typed words inside:

We can protect him.

We can ensure his abilities are nurtured safely.

Or we can remove him from danger.

Choose wisely.

Marcus folded the paper slowly.

"It means," he said quietly, "we're not alone anymore."

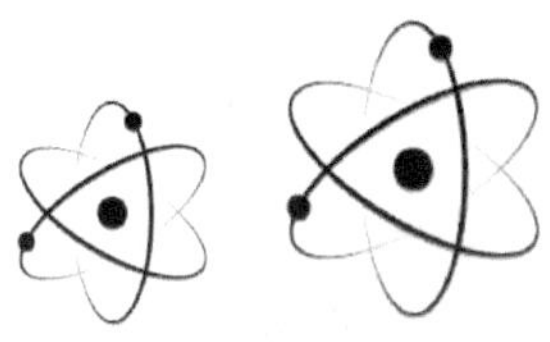

CHAPTER 9

Restless

Sleep refused the Freemans that night.

Janelle sat in the living room, a thin blanket draped over her shoulders, the envelope from the suited man clutched in her hands. She read it again. And again. Each word grew heavier, like the paper itself was pressing into her chest.

Marcus kept pacing the hall, checking doors, windows, even the basement. His hands were raw from gripping locks, his eyes darting to every shadow as if the walls themselves might hold someone.

"Do you think they're still out there?" Janelle asked, her voice barely a whisper.

Marcus stopped at the window, scanning the street. The SUV was gone, but the memory remained, crawling along the edges of his thoughts. "I don't know," he said.

"But yeah."

"They're watching."

Above them, Elian shifted in his sleep. A quiet spill of words left his mouth – broken phrases of Zulu. Each whisper from his room made Janelle's heart jump.

"I don't want them to take him," she muttered, more to herself than to Marcus.

Marcus joined her, resting a hand on the back of the couch. "They won't. We'll do whatever it takes." He hesitated, eyes flicking toward the staircase. "But we've got to be careful. These aren't just strangers. They're trained. And they know what they're looking for."

The house creaked around them, every sound amplified. The shadows in the corner deepened, though the room was lit. Marcus felt as though the walls themselves were watching.

Listening.

Elian murmured again upstairs.

Janelle turned her head sharply. "Do you think...he feels them?"

Marcus didn't answer. He had noticed little changes before: how the boy's skin sometimes shimmered at the wrong moment, or how his body vibrated faintly when no one else was near.

They both knew without speaking that the envelope was

only the beginning.

The outside eyes were patient.

Waiting.

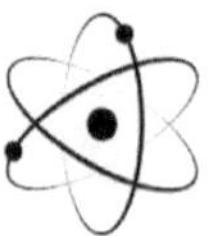 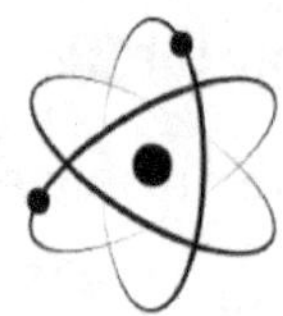

CHAPTER 10

The Doorway

The room at Grady Hospital was unchanged. Dull walls, a cracked chair, a buzzing lamp that flickered when no one touched it.

Xinavane hadn't asked for anything different.

From her satchel, she drew a small cloth pouch, loosening the string with careful fingers. A pleasant earthy smell drifted out – dried herbs, ground roots. She sprinkled a pinch into a shallow bowl of water, swirling it until the surface formed a small vortex.

Marcus watched, arms crossed but eyes hopeful.

Janelle lingered by the doorway, face set in suspicion.

Elian sat on the chair again, tense but not as rigid as before. His eyes swung to the bowl, then to Xinavane. "What's that?"

"Memory," Xinavane said simply. She knelt so her eyes were level with his. "When I was your age, my grandmother sang me through storms. She told me water remembers every sound it has ever touched." She gestured gently to the bowl. "Tonight, it will remember you."

He frowned, not understanding, but something in her tone kept him quiet.

Xinavane began to hum. Low at first, a ribbon of sound winding through the air. The hum deepened into a rhythm – half lullaby, half prayer, words slipping between Zulu and English. She rocked gently as she sang, her hands tracing slow arcs in the air.

Elian's breathing slowed. His shoulders dropped. The faint vibration beneath his skin softened, as though something inside him had leaned back.

"Close your eyes," Xinavane whispered.

He obeyed.

"What do you see?"

Elian's brow furrowed. His voice was small, distant.

"A hallway. Long. The walls are moving."

Marcus stiffened, instinctively stepping forward, but Xinavane lifted a hand without breaking rhythm.

"It's alright. You are safe. Walk a little further."

Elian's lips trembled. "There are doors. Too many. They keep changing."

Xinavane's hum deepened further, the rhythm steady. "Find the one that feels like yours. Put your hand on it."

Silence stretched.

Elian's breath hitched.

Then, in the waking world, his hand lifted slowly. It hovered in the air, pressing against something only he could feel.

Janelle gasped.

Xinavane's eyes stayed locked on the boy.

"Yes," Xinavane whispered. "Good."

Her voice sharpened, just slightly. "Now…open it."

Elian's body jolted. His eyes snapped open.

The bowl of water shuddered, its surface rippling violently before going completely still.

And somewhere between breaths, the space around Elian thinned — as if the room itself was expanding to make room for what was coming next. For a split second, the chair beneath him seemed to melt, its frame looked as though he sat both on it and inside it.

Then it was gone.

He sagged back, panting, tears streaking his face.

"I did it," he managed. "I touched it."

Marcus knelt beside him, his hands on Elian's shoulders. "You did it, son! You did it."

Janelle's lips parted, but no words came out. She pressed her hands to her chest, torn between awe and dread.

Xinavane sat back slowly, her hum fading. Her expression was calm, but her eyes burned with something fiercer – recognition – maybe even relief.

"You've found the door," she told Elian softly.

"Next time, we'll see what's on the other side."

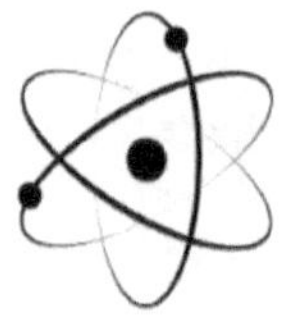

CHAPTER 11

Whispers in the Hall

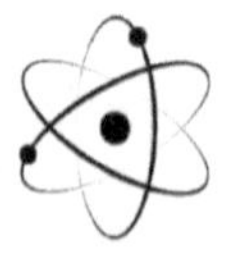

Grady's corridors had their own kind of gravity. They pulled secrets down them like a current, dragging every whispered story from one wing to another. By morning, what happened in one room could be reshaped, embroidered, and passed like gospel in the cafeteria line.

Elian Freeman had become a current all his own.

Nurses swapped stories in the break room – how he'd been found fused into a wall, how he'd mumbled in strange tongues while sedated. A young resident swore he saw the boy's hand blur during an IV insertion. Another nurse rumored that maybe the boy wasn't sick at all, maybe he was possessed.

Dr. Henry hated every word of it.

He paced down the hall with long, decisive strides, white

coat trailing, stethoscope bouncing on his chest like a badge. Rumors were a cancer, and in his hospital, he cut them out. The Freeman boy was a medical case – a complicated, bizarre one, sure, but nothing more. And yet ever since that foreign hypnotist had shown up, the air around the boy had become polluted with – nonsense.

He spotted her easily through the glass of Elian's room.

Dr. Xinavane Medousa stood tall and poised, her hands resting lightly on the arm of the boy's chair as she spoke in a voice meant only for him. The parents looked on, nervous but trusting.

Henry clenched his jaw.

Trust – that was a problem.

The Freemans were desperate, and desperate families were easy prey for charlatans. He'd seen it before. Energy healers, faith surgeons, "alternative" specialists who swooped in with mystical promises and left behind only disappointment and wreckage.

When Xinavane stepped out into the hall, Henry intercepted her.

"Dr. Medousa, isn't it?" His voice was polite, but edged.

She lifted her head. "Yes." Her voice was soft yet heavy, precise but patient.

"I understand you're...working with the Freeman boy."

Her gaze met his evenly. "I am helping him access parts of

his mind the hospital cannot reach."

"That's one way of putting it." Henry crossed his arms. "You're not licensed here. You're not on staff. You've bypassed every channel of oversight this hospital has."

Her lips curved – not a smile, exactly, more an acknowledgement. "Oversight has not cured him."

The simplicity of the statement infuriated him.

"What you're doing may not be safe. Hypnosis in an unstable child? Introducing untested cultural rituals? You're interfering in active treatment."

Xinavane didn't shrink or flinch. She only tilted her head, studying him like a surgeon examining an X-ray.

"And yet you are afraid," she said quietly.

He stiffened. "Excuse me?"

"You've seen it too," she continued, her voice low enough that only he could hear. "The way he vibrates. The way the air bends near him. You tell yourself it's stress, or drugs, or faulty observation. But part of you knows. And that part keeps you awake at night."

For a moment, Henry's composure cracked. His feelings betrayed his face – denial, anger, maybe fear. Then he snapped his coat closed and straightened.

"This is my hospital," he said tightly. "And if you put that boy at risk, I'll make sure you're escorted out of here."
"Permanently."

Xinavane raised her head again, calm as stone. "Then we shall see whose truth endures longer – yours, or his."

She stepped past him, her presence leaving a hush in her wake. Henry watched her go, fists balled tight in his pocket.

Around them, the hospital whispered on.

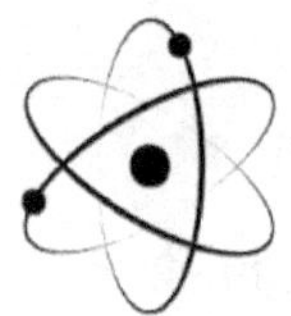

CHAPTER 12

Between Two Worlds

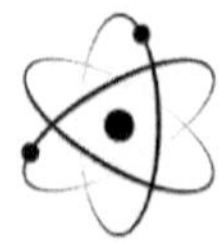

Sleep had never been so safe for Elian.

He feared it the way other children feared dark basements or thunderstorms. Closing his eyes meant surrendering to something bigger than himself — something that pulled at him from inside, like gravity from another direction.

But this night was different.

After Xinavane's quiet lullaby and the gentle rhythm of her voice, sleep came faster than expected. His head fell heavy against the pillow, the chirping of the machines fading, the hospital walls dissolving into shadow.

And then —

He was standing in his own bedroom.

The blue dinosaur lamp glowing on the dresser, the quilt

Janelle had sewn lay folded at the foot of the bed. Everything was familiar – but changing. The air was wet. Edges melted. Lines bled. The room looked as if it had been painted in watercolors and left too long in the rain.

He stepped forward, and the floor rippled under his foot.

The wall across from him thinned, then vanished. For a moment, he saw through it – not just into the hallway, but into another space, layered on top of the familiar. A street he didn't know, dusky sky overhead, figures moving like shadows under ice. The two realities overlapped, each one only half solid.

"Elian..."

The voice came from everywhere and nowhere. Not Janelle's. Not Marcus's. Older – like many voices braided into one.

"Who's there?" he whispered.

The air shifted.

Suddenly, he was in both places at once – his room and the street, his quilt and the shadows, his nightstand and the night sky. His body stretched painfully, as if two versions of him were being pulled apart. His chest constricted. His arms trembled, reshuffling in and out of reality.

Something moved in the overlapping street.

A figure stepped toward him – tall, faceless, its body blurred like a smear of wet paint dragged across glass. The closer it came, the colder his bones felt, like ice beneath his skin.

"Elian," the layered voice said again, deeper this time. *"Choose."*

His knees buckled. "Choose what?"

The figure raised its hand, and the world split down the middle like torn film.

His bedroom peeled away. The hospital monitors beeped in the distance, muffled, while the other world – the darker one – glared bright and sharp, filled with impossible angles and colors his eyes weren't made to see.

He staggered, caught between the two, the floor dissolving under his feet.

Then he heard another voice. Softer. Familiar.

"Elian, stay with me."

Xinavane.

Her words penetrated through the dream, driving light between the two realities. He clung to it like a rope, bracing himself as the figure dissolved into smoke. The torn film sealed shut, and his bedroom reassembled around him in shaky fragments.

He woke gasping, sweat slick across his forehead, the hospital room pressing down in heavy silence.

Janelle stirred in the chair beside his bed.

But for a heartbeat longer, Elian saw the light still clinging to the walls – like the world wasn't finished choosing which version of itself to be.

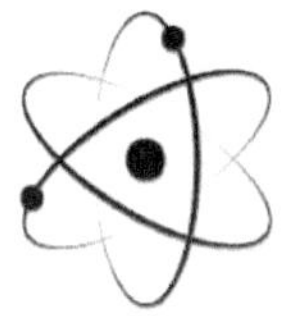

CHAPTER 13

The Invisible

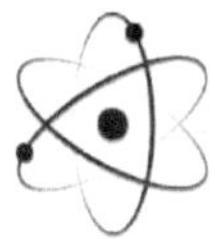

Elian woke before the sun, chest tight, heart still pounding from the dream he didn't dare speak aloud.

He lay still on the hospital bed, staring at the ceiling tiles, tracing the rigid lines with his eyes. The overlapping street and bedroom from the night before hung from the edge of his vision. He blinked, tried to will it away. Still, for a fraction of a second, he felt both worlds tugging at him at once.

Marcus came in first, coffee in hand, tired smile already forming. "Morning, champ," he said, pausing for a sip. "How'd you sleep?"

Elian shrugged, eyes fixed upward. "Fine," he muttered.

"Fine?" Marcus crouched beside the bed, forcing Elian to look at his father. "You've been having nightmares again?"

Elian shook his head and looked back at the ceiling. "Just...dreams."

Janelle arrived moments later, worry etched deep in her features. "You look drained, baby – hungry?"

"I'm fine," Elian said again. His voice was too even, too practiced.

Xinavane appeared behind them, as quiet as a shadow, a small notebook tucked beneath her arm. She smiled at Elian. He didn't return it.

Her calm presence brushed against him, like a hand on the back of his mind, and yet he recoiled inwardly.

"You slept well?" she asked.

He nodded once, eyes still fixed above. "Yes."

She sat beside him, folding her hands over her knees. "Good. Today, we'll continue...slowly. Nothing more than observation."

Elian's chest loosened slightly, but a quiet tension lingered. He didn't tell her about the street, or the figure, or the choice he'd been asked to make. He couldn't. He barely understood it himself. Instead, he held on to one thing – the memory of her voice threading through the chaos, reassuring him. That much he could trust.

That much he kept.

The day passed routinely: medications, vitals, dressing changes, bloodwork.

Staff lingered too long outside his room.

Whispers followed Xinavane down the hall.

Elian felt it all. The watching. The bending of the world when he closed his eyes.

And still, he said nothing.
Not yet.

For now, he carried it inside. A secret pull in his mind, stretching him thin between worlds.

And somewhere in the back of his consciousness, a small, stubborn thought took root:

If I learn to walk there, I might never be afraid again.

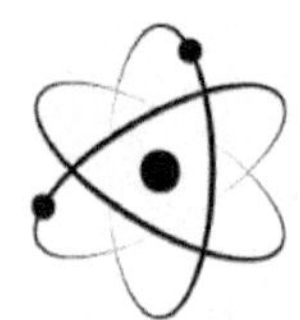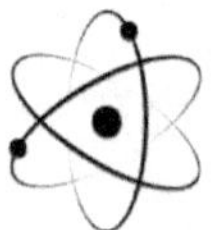

CHAPTER 14

First Steps Through

The hospital room was soundless. No machines. No loud-speakers. No staff.

Elian sat at the head of the bed, knees drawn to his chest. Xinavane sat at the foot.

Janelle and Marcus both stood near the doorway, stress knotted tight in their stomachs.

"Close your eyes," Xinavane said, her tone firm yet some-how gentle, like a drumbeat echoing somewhere deep in his chest. "Feel your body where it touches the bed. Imagine it...liquefying. Like water."

Elian hesitated, jaw tight. He felt the pull of the world around him – the firmness of the mattress, the walls, the floor – but beneath it all, he remembered the split street and room from the dream.

He clenched his fists, nervous. "I don't want to get stuck."

"You won't," Xinavane assured him. "I'll guide you. Just a small step. One wall. One breath."

He closed his eyes. The air thickened. His body felt heavy and light at the same time, as if gravity couldn't decide where he belonged.

"Focus your hand," Xinavane persisted. "Feel it. See it. And let it...slide.''

Elian raised his arm slowly, shaking, hand quivering. His body rippled faintly. The tip of his fingers blurred, edges dissolving, passing halfway through the mattress as though the fabric were water.

Janelle gasped, hands flying to her mouth. "Oh my God..."

"It's okay," Xinavane promised. "Good. Keep breathing. Pull it back when you're ready."

Heart racing, he drew it out inch by inch, gasping as the bed snapped back solid beneath him.

"I did it," he said, voice trembling in awe.

"Yes," Xinavane said, eyes bright. "You found the frequency. You controlled it. That is the first step."

Marcus rushed forward, cupping his son's face. "That was incredible, son!"

Janelle stepped closer, tears welling. "Elian..." her voice broke, a mixture of fear, relief, and wonder.

Elian blinked, his reality still fuzzy like a half-formed memory. For a moment, he felt the thrill of possibility – the power to move, to exist, to choose.

Xinavane noted the delicate shift. He was no longer a passenger in his own mind. He had tasted control.

The first small steps had been taken.

And somewhere outside the walls of this room, forces that would take notice were beginning to stir.

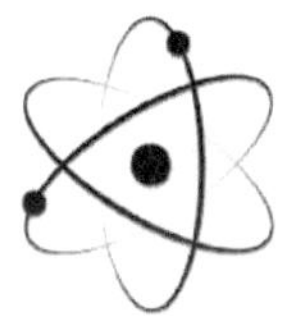 

CHAPTER 15

Testing the Boundaries

The hospital had become a laboratory of rumors and possibilities.

Xinavane stood across from Elian, her posture relaxed. But her eyes alert, always scanning, always aware. The boy perched on the edge of the bed, brimming with anticipation.

"Remember, control, not speed," Xinavane said softly. "Sense the boundaries before you cross them. Be certain. You are anchored, even when you float."

Elian nodded, swallowing hard.

His first attempt yesterday had been small – a hand through a mattress – but today, he wanted more. He wanted to see what his body could really do.

He closed his eyes – felt the pull in his chest, the light tug of the walls, the hum of the room.

Xinavane's voice wove through his mind with guided imagery. "Breathe. Slide through slowly. One wall. Only one."

He pushed forward. First, the air around his fingers, then the knuckles, then the entire arm, dissolving into a soft, translucent blur. The wall accepted him without resistance.

"Yes, now step," Xinavane insisted.

Elian hesitated.

Then, summoning every ounce of courage, he moved his torso forward. His body blurred, and then – he was inside the wall.

He could feel the other side, smell the sharp, sterile air in the hallway beyond, see the shadowy outline of a nurse moving past just outside his reach.

Without thinking, he pulled back.

The wall released him, and he slid into solid space again.

"I did it!" His voice shaky with exhilaration. "I...I really did it!"

Marcus and Janelle were silent for a moment, stunned, then...Marcus laughed – raw, relieved. "That's my boy!"

Janelle's hand trembled as she gripped the bedrail. "But...that's impossible."

Xinavane smiled confidently. "Nothing about him is impossible. He is learning how to navigate his own thresholds."

Outside the hospital, other thresholds were being crossed.

A private bio-tech firm – **Covenant Dynamics** – had taken notice.

Reports of the "Atlanta boy" with the impossible condition had reached their research division within hours. Analysts debated the potential:

Genetic anomaly? Psychic mutation? Or something else entirely?

Dr. Henry, already suspicious of Xinavane, found his inbox flooded with emails flagged "**URGENT: Patient Freeman case – Review.**"

Covenant Dynamics was officially involved.

Meanwhile, a black SUV sat idling across the street from Grady. Inside, three men in suits watched the building, one of them tapping a tablet, scrolling through biometric graphs.

"The subject is advancing faster than predicted," said one. *"He may be ready for the Phase Program sooner than anticipated."*

A chill ran down Xinavane's spine that evening as she left the hospital.

She had felt the energy shift – another presence, like eyes on Elian that didn't belong to any parent or nurse.

She didn't yet know the full extent, but she recognized it. She had seen these people before in South Africa. Children with gifts disappearing into government hands. Some never returned.

"We need to move carefully," she muttered to herself.

"They're coming."

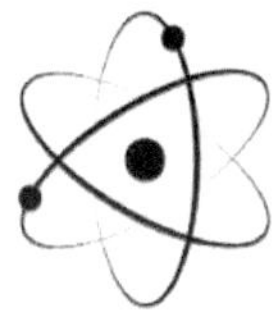

CHAPTER 16

The Hunt

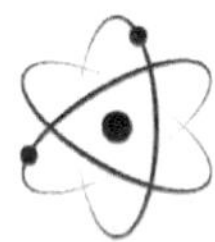

Xinavane had been in hospitals long enough to know when the question was real.

Most people in Grady asked with worry, or angst, or anxiety – where is the pharmacy, how long was the wait, was their loved one still breathing?

But the man in the gray suit asked differently.

He moved through the corridors with a predator's patience. His voice softened to something that pretended to be harmless. The agent had been circling the wards all morning, stopping orderlies and receptionists, leaning in close with questions he thought sounded casual:

Had anyone seen a boy named Elian?

About nine or ten.

Quiet. Sometimes sickly.

Adoptive parents, African American.

Checked in recently, unusual case.

The clerk shook her head, distracted by a ringing phone. The man smiled, too polite, too patient.

Xinavane, seated a few chairs down in the waiting area, heard every word.

This wasn't a man idly curious. This was a hunter on familiar ground. He wasn't just searching, he was narrowing in.

When he peeled away from the desk, Xinavane adjusted her coat and slipped through the crowd, trailing him, falling into step at a safe distance.

At the nurse's station, he leaned across the counter, flashing something that was meant to be official. The badge was too new, the laminated edges still stiff. Xinavane saw the nurse's hesitation, her quick glance toward the security desk, but before she could decide, the agent reeled his charm back in, softened his tone, and left her *just* uncertain enough to do nothing.

That was their method.

Never force. Never rush.

Just enough pressure to open a door.

Xinavane had seen enough. The way his hand hovered near his coat pocket, the calculated angle of his feet. The way his eyes lingered on the pediatric wing's double doors.

Elian's floor.

A chill crawled across her skin. She whispered a word in her mother tongue, grounding herself.

This wasn't coincidence.

This was the first sign of something bigger.
Something sinister.

The agent had found Grady. And now, inevitably, he would find Elian.
Unless she moved first.

He scanned faces, corners, exits. When his eyes drifted too close to hers, she turned into a side hallway, hiding behind a linen cart. She wasn't ready to confront him – not here, not with so many witnesses.

Still, she didn't lose him.

He crossed into the cafeteria for coffee.

Xinavane quickened her pace toward the entrance, footsteps swallowed by the noise of machines and voices.

This was her chance.

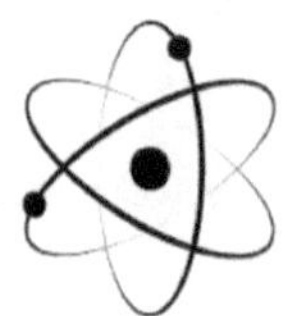 

CHAPTER 17

Catch and Release

The cafeteria was nearly empty — a few orderlies with plastic trays, a television hissing in the corner.

He chose a booth in the back.

Perfect.

Xinavane crossed the room and slid into the seat across from him as if they were old friends. He blinked, startled, then carefully rebuilt his neutral expression.

"Excuse me," he began.

"You're looking for Elian."

The words stopped him cold.

His jaw tightened, his hands flexed on the table. "I don't know what you..."

"Don't waste your lies on me." She leaned forward, her tone shifting into a measured cadence she had spent years perfecting, each syllable a step down into the dark well of his mind. "You're tired. You've walked these halls all morning. You want to close your eyes, just for a moment."

His protest faltered.

His eyes slipped out of focus, caught by the rhythm of her words, the gravity of her stillness. Xinavane's eyes did not waver; she held him as surely as if her hand were on his throat.

"Listen to me," she whispered, her words slid deeper, threading themselves through the narrow corridors of his thoughts. "You've been sent here to find Elian. Tell me – by whom?"

The man's lips parted, resistance trembling. Then, slowly, words spilled.

"We are called many things," he murmured. "Covenant Dynamics is one, Phasekeepers are another. We track the anomalies...bring them in for...containment."

Her gut tightened, though her face betrayed nothing.

Phasekeepers.

The old name, alive again.

"What do you do with them?" she pressed.

"They...test. Build the space. Keep them where they cannot...slip." His voice thinned, as though speaking the truth was draining him dry.

Silence pooled between them.

Around them, trays clattered. The television murmured. No one noticed.

She reached into his gaze one last time. "You will forget me. You will leave Grady. If you return, you will not ask about Elian again."

He nodded slowly, eyes glassy, emptied of intent.

When she stood, he remained motionless, staring into his untouched coffee.

Xinavane walked away without looking back.

The weight of what she had learned pressed down on every step. Stepped on every nerve.

The Phasekeepers were not just watching; they were already here.

And they would not stop.

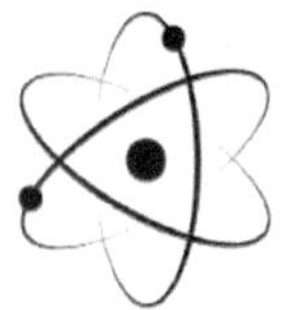

CHAPTER 18

The Bait and Switch

The elevator groaned as it climbed, each floor crawling past slower than the last. Xinavane stood between Janelle and Marcus, her voice low, controlled, her hands clenched at her sides.

"I have something to tell you," Xinavane confessed.

Janelle turned to her. "What is it?"

Xinavane didn't circle the point. "There's a man in the hospital. He is not staff. He's an agent – asking about Elian by name. I confronted him. He works for them – the Phasekeepers. They sent him here to gather information, not to take Elian. I made sure he won't remember a thing. But others –"

"*Others*?" Marcus interrupted. "You mean there are more of them here?"

"Possibly," she said. "They move in layers. The one I caught might have been —"

The elevator chimed, cutting her off.

The doors slid open to the pediatric floor.

Janelle stepped out first. "I just want to see my boy. Please, can we —"

She stopped.

The hallway outside Elian's room was wrong.

Empty. Too quiet.

The nurse's station unmanned. A single cup of coffee sat half-finished beside a glowing monitor.

Xinavane's skin went cold. "Stay here," she said, already moving.

She pushed Elian's door open and froze.

The bed was empty.

The sheets were pulled back neatly, as if he had simply gotten up and left. The heart monitor still motioned, tracing a rhythm that no longer had a body.

For a moment, none of them moved.

Then Janelle's scream tore through the room.

"Elian! Elian!"

Marcus rushed to the bed, ripping at the sheets as if the boy might somehow be hidden beneath them. The sound of his wife's voice broke him. He turned on Xinavane, fists trembling, eyes crazy. "You said he was safe! You said you stopped them!"

Xinavane's breath shook, but her mind raced faster than her fear. The scent of antiseptic hung heavy in the air — too heavy, masking something else beneath it.

Sedative.

She touched the IV port, still warm from use. The needle had been removed cleanly. Professional.

Her voice fell to a whisper. "The agent I hypnotized...he wasn't the hunter. He was the lure."

Janelle fell to her knees beside the bed, sobbing into the sheets. Marcus backed against the wall, his anger collapsing into silence.

Xinavane forced her thoughts into motion. The agent's surrender had been too easy. Too rehearsed.

We track the anomalies... bring them in for containment.

"They wanted me distracted," she whispered.

She moved to the window — open just a sliver. A cool draft brushed her cheek. Outside, the ambulance bay glowed beneath white floodlights. A single van was pulling away, unmarked, too clean for hospital transport.

"Marcus," she said quietly, "they've taken him."

He stared at her in disbelief. "Then get him back."

Xinavane met his stare, her own voice hardening to steel. "I will."

She tore the hospital badge from her coat, snapping the plastic in her fist. "They think they've stolen a sleeping child. What they've really done is awaken me."

Outside, the van disappeared into the Atlanta night.

And for the first time since her arrival, Xinavane felt the old current stir in her blood – the one she'd buried years ago, after Limpopo, after the disappearances, after her sister's screams.

It was happening again.

And this time, she would not let it end the same way.

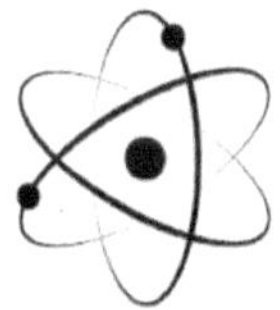

CHAPTER 19

The Escape

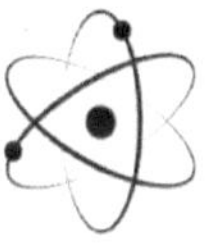

Elian woke to motion.

At first, he thought it was another dream — the hum of the tires beneath him, the vibration running through his spine.

He tried to move.

His hands wouldn't obey.

A soft restraint bit his wrists.

He opened his eyes fully.

The van's interior glowed a dim blue from a strip of light running across the ceiling. Cabinets lined one wall. Across from him sat two figures in gray uniforms, their faces masked, their movements silent.

Not EMTs.

Elian's throat burned when he tried to speak.

"Where...are you taking me?"

Neither answered.

One of them glanced at a small monitor built into the wall — a pulse line moving in time with Elian's heartbeat.

"Subject stable," the man said quietly. "No phase distortion yet."

Elian's heart skipped.

Phase.

The word cracked something open in his chest. He remembered the last time it happened — the last time he "phased" — the way the world softened around him, how the bed begun to sink into his body, or maybe the other way around.

He thought that Xinavane had helped him to control it — that it happened because of the dreams.

But now he felt it again.

The air inside the van wavered.

He blinked. The walls pulsed faintly. The guards didn't notice; they never did at first.

Elian focused on the sounds of the van: the hum of the tires, the vibration beneath his back. His breathing slowed.

He remembered Xinavane's words, the ones she used in her sessions: *You are not trapped by the phase; you are its pulse. You decide when and where.*

He swallowed hard, closing his eyes.

The restraints on his wrist began to change – half liquid, half solid.

"Hey!" one of the guards shouted. "He's destabilizing!"

Elian's eyes snapped open. Inside the van, the colors bled from silver to deep violet. For a moment, the world lost its edges.

And then he saw them.

Shadows. Not reflections, not shapes. Presences – pressed into the corners of the van. They moved like smoke caught in glass, whispering in a language he didn't know, but some-how recognized.

The guards reached for syringes, their motions frantic.

Elian didn't move.

He let the current rise.

His body vibrated, humming with that strange energy that always came before the shift.

He remembered Xinavane's hand on his chest, her voice steady: *When the world feels too thin, anchor to something real.*

His mother's face. His father's laugh. The warmth of the hospital light.

He reached for that memory – and the van dissolved around him.

For an instant, he was falling through light.

Then the world snapped sideways.

Silence.

Cold air.

Wet pavement soaked his hospital gown as he landed hard on his back.

Elian gasped, his body solid again, the night spinning above him. The van was gone, but not yet out of earshot – and the whispering shadows lingered at the edge of his vision, haunting him.

He had escaped.

But he wasn't alone.

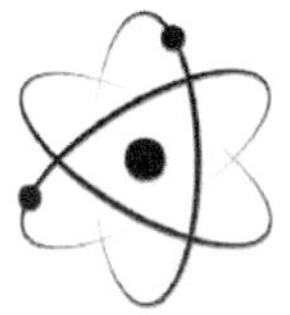

CHAPTER 20

The Concrete Jungle

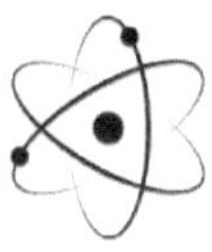

The world had never felt so loud.

Elian sprinted down an unfamiliar street, his hospital gown flapping against the cold Atlanta wind, bare feet slapping wet asphalt. The city glowed and throbbed around him. Streetlights buzzing, distant sirens, airbrakes, car horns — every sound scraped against his nerves.

He pressed a hand to his chest, steadying his breath.

Control is focus. Find your pulse. Find your place.

Xinavane's words felt far away.

His thoughts tangled — the van, the restraints, the men in gray. The whispering shadows that had followed him through the phase.

He glanced over his shoulder.

The street was empty. Still, he felt watched.

At the far end of the block, a sign flickered: **24-Hour Market.** The neon *r* blinked erratically. He pushed through the door, a bell jangled overhead.

A bored cashier glanced up. "Yo, kid, you okay? You look…"

"I just need water," Elian muttered, voice hoarse.

He moved to the cooler, grabbed a bottle, and twisted the cap with shaking fingers. The cold hit his throat like glass, but it cleared his head enough to think.

They'll come for you again.

He knew it.

The Phasekeepers didn't stop after one failure. They would trace the residue of his passage and follow the ripples he'd left behind.

Xinavane had warned him – phasing without focus left a mark. A scent in the air.

He needed to move.

He dropped the empty bottle on the counter. "I'll pay later," he mumbled.

"Hey—" the cashier called.

Elian was already gone.

Outside, the wind carried the smell of rain and exhaust. Somewhere nearby, a MARTA train groaned along its tracks.

He moved fast through alleyways and half-lit streets, past a mural of a bird frozen mid-flight, its wings fractured across the brick.

He slowed.

The paint started pulsing.

"Breathe," he whispered.

A thin vibration ran through him — the warning tremor before a phase. The mural's edges shimmered. Colors deepened. The world began to bend.

"No. Not now."

He tried to anchor himself — Xinavane's voice, his parent's faces — but panic scattered his thoughts.

Footsteps.

Two figures emerged from the shadow of the intersection.

Gray uniforms.

Stillness.

Elian's pulse spiked. He backed away, heels striking the curb. The hum returned to his bones.

"Don't," one of the agents called softly, voice almost kind. "You'll hurt yourself if you try again. Just come with us."

Elian shook his head. "I'm not going anywhere with you."

The streetlight above him buzzed – then exploded.

Darkness swallowed the street.

Elian ran.

His bare feet struck puddles, scattering light from passing cars. He darted between dumpsters, into an alley. Heart racing, mind racing. His vision blurred – brick melting into shadow, rain turning into static.

He could feel the phase clawing its way up his spine.

His molecules wanted to scatter, his body begging to slip between worlds again.

He slammed his hand against the cold wall, grounding himself. "Focus," he whispered. "Find your pulse."

The sound of pursuit closed in.

He turned a corner – and stopped.

A figure stood there. Not an agent. A girl, wrapped in a heavy coat, eyes shining with an unnatural light. She smiled.

"You're just like the others."

"Who are you?" Elian asked.

"Someone who's been waiting for you. We've been hiding in the seams – the ones they couldn't catch."

Behind her, three more shapes stepped forward, slightly translucent.

Children.

And for the first time since the van, Elian didn't feel alone.

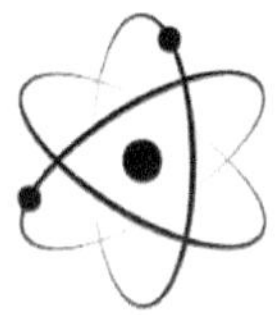

CHAPTER 21

The Others

The alley felt too still.

The rain should have echoed off the walls, but the sound seemed to die before it could reach him, as if the air itself refused to carry it.

Elian stared at the girl before him. Her coat was too big, sleeves hanging past her wrists, hair damp with drizzle. But her eyes — her eyes were unusual. They were the same color violet that appeared at the edges of his own vision when the world began to slip.

She studied him, unreadable.

"You phased out of containment," she said quietly. "That's not supposed to be possible."

Elian's voice cracked. "Who are you?"

She tilted her head, as though trying to decide whether to tell him the truth yet. "We're what happens when they fail."

The children behind her stepped closer. There were three – two boys and a girl, their outlines flickering slightly, as though their bodies couldn't decide how solid to be. One boy's face was half-shadowed, as if light refused to touch him. The smaller girl's feet barely brushed the ground.

"They said the Phasekeepers took everyone," Elian whispered.

"Xinavane said –"

At *that* name, the older girl's gaze sharpened. "You know Xinavane?"

"She helped me," he said. "She was supposed to keep me safe."

The girl exhaled – almost a laugh, but bitter. "Then she's still fighting. That's...something"

The world shifted.

For an instant, the alley vanished, replaced by a blurred corridor of glass and light – a memory not his own.

Elian staggered. "What was that?"

"The overlap," she said. "You're unstable. It happens after an uncontrolled shift. You're half in this world, half still echoing through their world."

"Their world?"

"The Phasekeepers," she said. "They build places between spaces. Liminal zones that only exist inside the phase. They trap kids like us there. Study us. Keep us from tearing the edges too wide."

The truth settled – slowly, heavy, unreal. "So...there are more of you?"

"Not so many anymore," said one of the boys.

Elian looked around. "Why did you save me?"

"We didn't," the girl replied gently. "We felt you. Every time someone phases near the surface, it shakes the seams. You shook them hard."

She took a step closer, her outline stabilizing, just enough for him to see the scar that ran along her temple.

"You're strong. Too strong for your age. That's why they came for you."

"They'll come again," Elian said.

"We know."

She reached out her hand. For a moment, he hesitated. Then he took it. Her skin was cool, but solid – real.

"Come with us," she said. "There's a place beneath the old freight tunnels where the city doesn't quite touch reality. It's safe there – For now."

Elian nodded.

Together they slipped deeper into the maze of alleys,

toward the sound of distant trains.

Elian glanced back once.

At the far end of the street, two Phasekeeper agents stood in the rain, motionless. One of them lifted a device that glowed violet.

"Elian," the girl cautioned, tugging his hand. "Don't look back."

He didn't.

They vanished into the dark.

And behind them, the city exhaled a low, metallic sigh, as though it too had seen enough to be afraid.

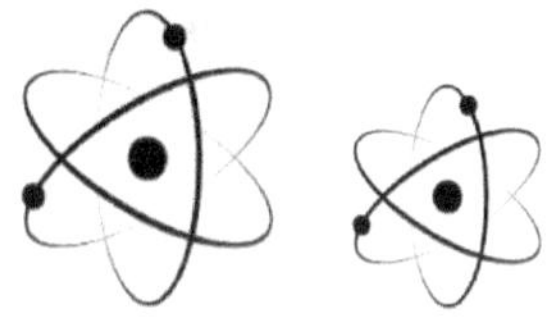

CHAPTER 22

Beneath the City's Skin

The tunnels breathed.

That was the first thing that Elian noticed — the air moved as if alive, exhaling warmth through the cracks in the stone. He followed the others down a slanted passage that dipped beneath the train yard, the girl with the oversized coat leading them with a steady hand pressed to the wall.

"Stay close," she warned. "The seams here are thin. If you drift, you slip."

Elian didn't ask what that meant. He could already feel it in his bones, like the world was vibrating a fraction too fast. Sometimes his vision blurred, and the tunnel became a different place entirely: metal corridors, white light, and echoes of people who weren't there.

They reached a point where the old subway tracks ended

abruptly. The girl knelt and brushed dust from the wall. Beneath it was a symbol drawn in chalk, barely noticeable. She pressed her palm to it.

The symbol glowed violet.

The wall opened.

On the other side lay the refuge.

It wasn't really a room, more like a pocket of warped space, stitched together from broken stations and forgotten doors. Children moved quietly between hammocks and dim lanterns. Some patched cracked pipes. Others sat cross-legged, eyes closed, glowing faintly as they swayed to something only they could hear.

"This is where we stay," the girl said. "Between the layers."

Elian stepped through as the wall sealed behind him with a soft sigh. "What is this place?"

"We call it the Fold," she replied, "It's what's left of us."

A boy, half-translucent, offered him a dented cup of water. "You shouldn't have made it here," he said. "Not alone."

Elian drank. The water was cold, but the taste was metallic. "I didn't mean to. They took me. I...slipped."

"Then you're lucky," said the girl. "Most people who slip don't come back."

A hum rolled through the floor, and everyone froze.

The lights dimmed. The walls wavered, like a flame in the

wind. Then the moment passed.

"They're searching," the girl said, frowning. "Every time they open a gate, we feel it."

Elian studied the others – tense, frightened, but practiced. This wasn't new to them.

He realized then, with a quiet chill, that they had lived this way for a long time.

Later, as the others drifted to sleep, he lay awake beneath a hanging tarp.

He thought of Xinavane – her calm voice, the certainty in her eyes when she said he was safe. He wanted to believe she was coming for him.

But as he stared into the darkness, another thought crept in.

What if this…this strange, breathing place beneath the streets wasn't a refuge at all?
What if it were another experiment? Another trap?

And then, somewhere deep in the Fold, a faint vibration began – movement in the seams, too subtle for anyone else to notice.

But Elian felt it.

A pulse…

A call…

A signal from somewhere beyond the Fold's edge.

He sat up slowly, violet light glowing in his eyes.

The city was speaking to him.

And it was calling his name.

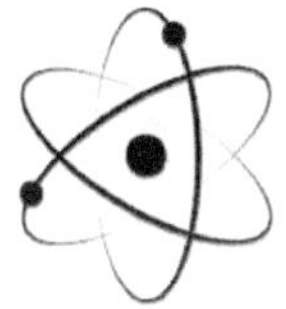 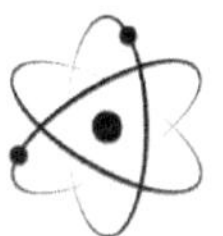

CHAPTER 23

Hi-Jacked

"Elian…"

He flinched and looked around. The others around him didn't stir. He closed his eyes.

The voice came again, patient, familiar.

Xinavane.

His heart lurched. He didn't know how he knew, but he did. The way her voice used to ground him in the hospital, calm and precise – it was that same tone, only stretched thin through static.

"I'm here," he whispered.

When he opened his eyes, she was there – not clearly, more like a reflection rippling across water. Her outline formed in violet light.

"Elian, stay where you are," the echo said. "I'm coming."

He reached out instinctively. His fingers brushed the air, and the whole chamber shuddered. Light splintered across the Fold like cracking glass.

The girl with the oversized coat was suddenly beside him, grabbing his wrist. "Stop!" she hissed.

He blinked, dazed. "She's trying to find me –"

"Exactly," the girl snapped. "And they're listening for her. You open the line, you open everything."

The others were waking up now, fear bright in their faces.

"Another trace?" one boy whispered.

The girl nodded. "A strong one."

"She's not one of them," Elian said desperately. "She saved me. She –"

"She trained them," the girl cut in. "Maybe once she helped. Maybe she didn't mean for it to go this far. But anyone emitting those types of frequencies, especially to communicate, is part of their net…whether they know it or not."

Tears burned Elian's eyes. "You don't understand. She's looking for me."

The girl's tone softened, just for a second. "I do. We all had someone looking for us once."

The light changed – and a deep violet pulse rolled through the tunnels. The walls bulged outward, then sank inward, as if the Fold itself was waking.

"She's close," one of the children said.

"No," the girl responded. "That's not her anymore. That's what's riding her signal."

Elian froze.

Through the static, the voice shifted – no longer calm, no longer Xinavane. He felt his skin prickle, the edges of his vision fuzzing into violet haze.

The girl gripped his shoulders. "Listen to me. Whatever you do, don't answer again."

He tried to nod, but the hum was too deep now – like a current pulling him inward. For a heartbeat, he saw flashes of Xinavane's face lit by rain, and behind her, something vast watching through her eyes.

Then the light collapsed.

Silence rushed back into the Fold.

Elian gasped for breath, clutching his chest. His pulse thundered in his ears.

"They've found a line," the girl whispered. "She's trying to reach you...but now they can reach her."

Elian stared at the blank wall where the light had been.

He didn't know if he'd just touched Xinavane's mind – or something wearing it.

Either way, the Fold was no longer safe.

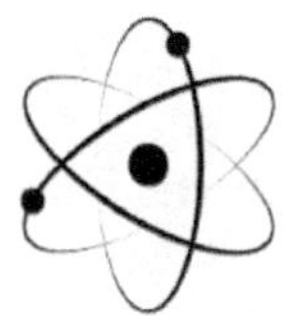

CHAPTER 24

The Voice Beneath the Static

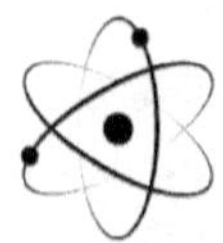

Xinavane hadn't slept for two days.

The hospital lights still burned behind her eyes when she blinked – sterile, white, useless. Every corridor she walked replayed itself in her mind: the agent she'd hypnotized, the illusion that fooled her, the boy taken from the very room she'd sworn to guard.

Now, in the dark of her apartment, she sat crossed-legged on the floor with a shallow bowl of water before her. The surface rippled into a rhythm that didn't come from her hands.

"Find him, find the thread," she chanted in her mother tongue.

Her voice was steady, but the space around her began to bend. The edges of her shadow broke into lines of color.

Then she felt it.

A pulse — soft at first, then rising — like a heartbeat traveling through stone. Elian's signature brushed her awareness. But it wasn't wild or panicked.

It was controlled.

He's learning, she realized. *Or someone is teaching him.*

Xinavane closed her eyes. The city unfolded inside her — power lines, rain-slick streets, the thrum of generators — all woven together by invisible currents. And beneath it all, faint but growing stronger, was him.

"Elian."

The name carried through the psychic tide.

The image shifted: a tunnel, children with glowing eyes, walls that breathed like lungs – a place folded beneath Atlanta's skin.

Xinavane's eyes snapped open. The bowl of water cracked.

Not containment. Not prison. Something else.

She moved fast, grabbing her satchel: notebook, inhaler, flask, and the small silver pendant her sister had given her before the first collapse in Limpopo.

The pendant pulsed once.

Deep violet.

The Fold.

She pulled on her coat and stepped into the rain.

Thunder rolled. The air tasted metallic — charged.

Then a voice brushed her mind.

"You shouldn't have followed him here."

Xinavane froze. The alley was empty — except for a brief shimmer, a suggestion of a figure that vanished as quickly as it appeared.

The Phasekeepers had felt her reaching.

She took a breath, clenched her fists, and let her mind open fully.

The rain lifted, suspended in midair for a heartbeat as she released a psychic pulse outward – a living sonar wave rippling through the city.

Every wall, every circuit, every heartbeat answered back.

And there he was.

Distant. Frightened.

Alive.

A beacon, burning inside the city's veins.

Her eyes glowed violet.

"Hold on, Elian," she whispered into the storm.

"I'm coming."

CHAPTER 25

The Breach

The earth quaked before the alarms began.

Elian was already running.

The Fold – the only place that had felt remotely safe – was falling apart. Walls shivered, light seeping through cracks, like trapped fire desperate to escape. The air buzzed, dense and low, making his teeth ache. Behind him, the children shouted as they scattered for the exits.

Nyari – the girl in the oversized coat – was pulling on a metal grate.

"This way!"

Elian turned just as the tunnel warped, folding in on itself. A section of the wall split open like fabric ripped by invisible hands.

Through it, figures stepped through.

Tall. Still. Faces hidden by translucent masks.

Phasekeepers.

"They're inside!" someone screamed.

"Go!" Nyari yelled.

Elian dove after her through the grate. The metal scraped his shoulders as he tumbled into a narrow service tunnel, water sloshing around his ankles. Behind them came sharp bursts of violet light — phasing weapons slicing through the dark like lightning.

One struck the wall inches from Elian's head.

The concrete turned to ash.

He slipped and caught himself on a rusted pipe. His hands flickered – solid, then not. The hum inside him surged, pulling his awareness sideways into flashes: white corridors of containment, a hand on a glass, rows of eyes watching.

"Stay grounded!" Nyari grabbed his wrist, forcing him to focus. Her grip was ice-cold.

"If you lose sync, they'll pull you through!"

He gave a shaky nod, his breath coming in ragged bursts.

A deep pulse surged through the tunnel – felt in the skull more than the ears, deeper than sound, more like a command. The water spread in rings like a shockwave. Somewhere behind them, they heard one of the children scream.

Nyari's face tightened. "They've anchored a gate. We're out of time."

They ran into a dead end. A rusted ladder led up toward a manhole where faint city light leaked through.

Nyari shoved him toward it. "Go!"

"What about you?"

"I'll collapse the tunnel. Move!"

Elian climbed, lungs burning as the sound of phasing bursts shook the tunnel below. He shoved the heavy manhole. It resisted — then gave way with a metallic groan.

Rain hit his face.

Night.

The city.

He pulled himself up onto the street, chest heaving. Traffic hissed past in the distance, oblivious. Beneath his feet, reality was tearing itself apart.

Nyari emerged seconds later, soaked and shaking. Behind her, the tunnel folded inward with a hollow implosion.

"Is it sealed?" Elian asked.

"For now," she said. "They'll reroute fast; we have to move."

They ran through side streets slick with rain, neon lights sliding across puddles.

"Elian," Nyari panted as they ducked under an awning. "Whatever you did. That connection you made? They traced it. They've got both your signatures now – yours and the doctor's."

"She's alive?"

"For now. But you're linked. If they get her, they get you."

The ground pulsed again – closer this time.

"They've triangulated," she whispered.

Elian looked at a shop window. In the reflection, three shadows condensed into shape — violet cores glowing.

"Run," Nyari said.

They did.

Through the storm, through a city that no longer felt real. The sound of pursuit followed – relentless, closing the distance one pulse at a time.

And then, through the noise of fear and thunder, a voice brushed Elian's mind.

"I'm still with you," the voice said.

Xinavane.

And for the first time since the hospital, hope flickered through fear, like a fragile candle in the dark.

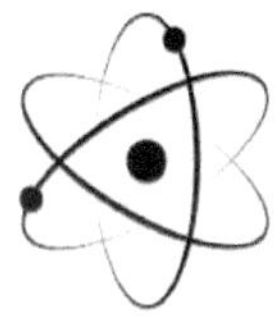

CHAPTER 26

You Can Run, But You Can't Hide

Rain hammered the streets like static.

Elian and Nyari darted down the sidewalk between two buildings, their breath visible in the cold. The hum behind them had not faded — it pulsed at steady intervals, like a sonar heartbeat mapping every corner they passed.

"This way," Nyari whispered, tugging his sleeve.

They turned down a service alley, cluttered with dumpsters and a flickering red light. A half-broken sign buzzed above them:

GRADY MAINTENANCE ACCESS

The irony wasn't lost on him — back where it started.

The alley ended at a loading door — closed but not locked.

Inside, the air was damp, stale – a forgotten sub-level maybe.

"Down here," Nyari said.

They hurried down a narrow stairwell into a hallway of broken lights that blinked like dying stars. The noise of the city drained away, replaced with a silence that felt...heavy.

"Where are we going?" Elian asked nervously.

Nyari didn't answer. She tilted her head, listening through the walls.

After a moment, she said, "They're not close yet. But they will be."

She guided him into a utility room. Rusted beds, scattered tools, and water-stained patient files littered the floor.

Elian collapsed against the wall, shaking. "I saw them," he whispered. "When I phased out of the Fold. They were testing people. Kids like us."

Nyari squatted beside him. "They've been doing it for years. I was one of the first they caught. The Fold wasn't built to protect us – it was built to *feed* off us."

He looked up, confused. "Feed?"

"The energy we make when we phase," she said. "They use it to stabilize their world. To keep their liminal spaces from collapsing on them."

A metallic clang echoed down the hall.

They both froze.

Nyari's eyes widened. "They found the access door."

"How many?" Elian whispered.

"Three. Maybe four."

Elian pushed himself upright. Every nerve buzzing. "Can you phase us out?"

"Not without burning this pocket of space to the ground. It would leave a trail they could follow."

"So, what do we do?"

She looked at the wall – cracked concrete, water seeping through its veins.

"We hide inside."

Before he could speak, she pressed her palm against the concrete. Her hand slipped through it like water.

"Hold your breath."

They stepped into the wall.

Time stretched thin.

Footsteps echoed from the other side – agents sweeping the perimeter, scanning, voices clipped from walkie-talkies.

Elian could see them through the concrete – three silhouettes outlined in violet, faces blurred into nothing.

One of them stopped.
Turned.

Faced the wall directly.

Elian tried not to breathe.

Nyari tightened her grip. *Don't move.*

The agent raised a device. It's hum deepened – the same frequency that made Elian's skin tingle and his bones vibrate.

They can sense us.

Nyari's eyes darted to his – panic flashing.

"Run," she breathed.

She yanked him back through the concrete. The world exploded into motion again – alarms, flashing lights, shouting voices.

They sprinted down another corridor, water splashing under their feet. A stairwell loomed ahead, leading up toward daylight.

"They're using you," she gasped. "You have to break the connection before they use it again."

"How?"

"By going deeper than they can reach."

He didn't understand – but there was no time to ask.

The stairwell shook as they climbed. Dust rained from above. The hum peaked – furious and close – no longer searching – now hunting.

They reached a maintenance door.

Rain pounded against it.

Nyari gripped the handle and looked at Elian. "When we run, don't look back. No matter what you hear."

She pulled the door.

Cold air. Thunder. Sirens.

They ran into the storm.

CHAPTER 27

The Hollow House

Rain fell in sheets, but they couldn't slow down.

The low, relentless hum followed them like a heartbeat under the city's skin.

Nyari led, her hair soaked and clinging to her face, eyes scanning between alleys.

They crossed into a quieter part of the city. Block after block of boarded-up row houses and abandoned warehouses. No sirens. No people.

Only the hum.

"There," she said finally, pointing toward a narrow house with warped shutters and no lights. "It's hollow."

Elian frowned. "Hollow?"

She didn't explain. She pushed the door open with her

shoulder. It gave easily, the sound lost in the storm.

Inside, the air smelled like rot and dust. Furniture lay hidden beneath sheets. Wallpaper peeling from the walls. It felt abandoned – yet somehow aware...alive.

Nyari closed the door slowly.

For the first time in hours, the hum fell silent.

Elian sagged against the wall, shaking. His hands trembled, flickering at the edges like static. "I can't shut it off," he whispered.

"The phasing?"

He nodded. "It's like – like part of me is still...in there."

"You're not out yet," she said. "The Fold doesn't just hold you – it marks you. It keeps trying to pull you back."

"Can we stop it?"

"We can run," she said. "Stopping it? That's something only the doctor can do."

At the thought of Xinavane, Elian felt her presence and then heard her voice in his mind:

"Hold on."

Elian pushed off the wall. "She's still out there."

Nyari's eyes shifted toward the window. "If you can feel her, they can too."

Elian followed her eyes.

Outside, through the rain-blurred glass, a car idled too long at the corner. Two figures stepped out.

Agents.

"They found us," Nyari whispered.

"How?"

"They always find their mark."

The house creaked, as if answering her.

"We can't phase again," she said. "They'll trace it. We hide."

They slipped behind the stairwell as the front door eased open.

Footsteps. Slow. Careful.

A flashlight beam swept across the dust.

Elian pressed his palm to the wall, trying to make himself still. The hum began to rise again, alive with pressure through his bones – the agents tuning in.

Nyari leaned close, her lips barely moving. "If they touch you, they can pull you through. Don't let them."

The footsteps drew closer.

A pause.

The beam of light passed inches from their hiding spot.

And then – from upstairs – a faint *bang*.

The agents turned toward it instantly, weapons raised.

"Now," she whispered.

They burst through the kitchen and out the back door. Rain crashing into them.

Behind them came shouts – and the hum surged – so powerful it rattled the air. Violet light flared.

In an instant, the house folded in on itself – walls bending, space collapsing – then it vanished like smoke.

They ran through the rain until their legs gave out, collapsing under an overpass.

Elian could hardly catch his breath. "That house –"

"Wasn't a house," Nyari said. "It was a breach."

"A…what?"

"A remnant of the Fold," she said. "A place where it bled through. And now it's spreading."

She looked up at the skyline, where distant lightning lit up the city, and for a second, she saw two cities overlapping: one real, one flickering just behind it.

Nyari's face hardened. "We're running out of time."

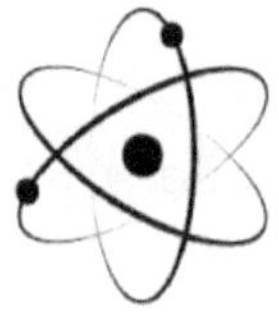

CHAPTER 28

The City Ghosts

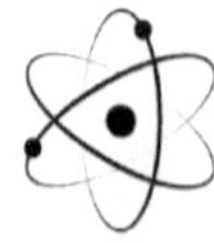

Elian and Nyari kept moving.

They climbed the overpass as mist swallowed the city below. Sirens wailed somewhere in the distance – dozens of them – echoing through the rain. Beneath it all was the hum.

Always the hum.

"Something's happening," Nyari said, as her pace slowed.

The skyline ahead pulsed violet, then black, then violet again. Windows lit up and went dark in strange sequences, reflecting streets that didn't exist.

Down below, traffic had stopped. People stood in the rain, staring upward, their own outlines stuttering – flickering in and out of reality.

One man stepped forward.

Half his body passed through a streetlight. He didn't scream. Didn't even react. Just kept walking.

Elian swallowed hard. "The Fold...it's inside them."

"No," Nyari said. "It surrounds them." She grabbed his arm. "We need to move before the frequency shifts again."

They crossed the overpass, heading toward Old Fourth Ward, where the lights were dimmer and the streets older. Every step felt heavier, like gravity itself couldn't decide where it belonged.

Then –

At the far end of the bridge, an explosion tore through the skyline. A burst of violet energy lit up the storm clouds from below.

A building several blocks away folded in on itself like crumpled paper...and vanished.

Screams cut through the rain.

"That's them," Nyari said. "They're stabilizing a breach. Anchoring the Fold to the city."

Elian felt cold spread through his chest. "They are turning *Atlanta* into a containment field."

Nyari didn't argue. She just ran.

They ducked into a narrow side street. The pavement beneath them began to ripple like liquid. From behind, the hum intensified.

Agents.

Three of them phased in at the far end of the street.

"Run!" Nyari shouted.

They raced through a maze of alleys. Every turn seemed to loop back on itself — geometry betraying them. Shadows stretched too far, whispers followed them.

"Elian — left!"

He skidded around the corner and froze. The street ahead wasn't a street anymore. It was a reflection — a perfect mirror image of where they had just been. The agents were there too, only facing the other direction.

Their reflections moved a second too late.

"What is this?" Elian stood petrified.

"The breach is widening. The Fold's overlaying real space."

The agents — both real and reflected turned toward them.

Elian's skin prickled; his pulse locked into the vibration in the air. The phasing started again, involuntarily. His body began blinking in and out of view; his eyes glowed violet.

"Don't phase!" Nyari shouted. "They'll trace you!"

"I can't stop it!"

He dropped to one knee, heaving, as reality buckled. Rain fell upward. The world skipped frames.

Then, in the middle of the distortion, he saw her.

Xinavane – standing in the ruins of a hospital corridor, hand outstretched.

Focus, Elian.

He reached for her hand – his body snapped back into alignment. His outline solidified just long enough for Nyari to drag him through a service door and slam it shut behind them.

Inside, darkness – the smell of oil and iron hung heavy in the air, pipes crawled along the walls like veins.

They leaned against the wall breathless.

Outside, the hum passed by slowly, searching – then moved on.

Nyari pressed her hand to her chest and whispered, "That wasn't just phasing, you synced with her."

Elian nodded slowly. "She's alive. She's fighting."

Nyari looked at him – fear and hope warring in her eyes. "Then she'd better move fast. Because the city's shifting."

Elian stared into the dark, listening to the thunder. No...not thunder – the sound of the Fold spreading, synchronizing.

Atlanta was phasing in and out of existence, flickering between real and folded – building by building, block by block.

The Fold was no longer a cage.

It was becoming a mirror.

A reflection that could replace the original.

The end of separation.

The rise of the in between.

CHAPTER 29

Secrets Beneath Grady

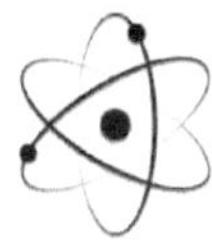

The elevator doors opened to a floor that didn't exist on any hospital blueprint.

No signage. No floor number.

Xinavane stepped out, flashlight in one hand, pulse sensor in the other. The air pressed in around her; a buzzing was at the edge of her hearing. It wasn't electricity – it was resonance. The same frequency that lived inside Elian.

She followed the trail through sealed access doors and unmarked stairwells, past storage wards long abandoned. Each level grew quieter, until even the hospital's mechanical noises: vents, oxygen lines, even distant footsteps, faded away.

The place was sealed off.

A chain of fluorescent lights hung overhead. One bulb worked, blinking in a slow rhythm.

Xinavane stopped beneath it, listening. The vibration wasn't random. It matched a biological frequency.

Elian's frequency.

She pressed the sensor to the wall. A reading flashed, then spiked – **massive energy fluxes** below.

Something was alive down there.

She walked further, boots echoing softly.

Machines lined the corridor, half covered by tarps. Containment pods cracked open. Each pod marked with a serial tag:

P-03 SUBJECT STATUS – PHASE UNSTABLE
P-07 SUBJECT STATUS – NULL DRIFT DETECTED

She stopped at one labeled P-09.

The tarp had fallen away completely. Inside lay a small hospital bed – restraints cut.

The mattress was scorched.

And the wall behind it was gone.

In its place, a perfect circular void – smooth, silent, iridescent edges.

It wasn't a portal.

It was a scar on reality.

Xinavane stepped closer. The air pulled strands of light from her fingertips.

"Show me what you've done," she whispered.

She reached out, just enough to graze the edge of the void.

Instantly, images flashed through her – not visions, but data memories, stored impressions in the Fold: Children being tested, restrained, monitored by agents in Phasekeeper suits.

Elian screaming in his sleep as instruments glitched around him. Nyari in a dark room, whispering through a wall to someone unseen.

Then, deeper still – a presence she recognized but didn't understand. Something vast. Watching. Learning.

She tore her hand back, gasping. The hum grew angry now. Resonating through metal beams and concrete.

From behind, a voice spoke – smooth, precise, too calm for a place like this. "You shouldn't be here, Doctor."

Xinavane turned.

A man in a dark suit stepped from the shadows, badge flashing silver for a split second before he tucked it away.

"You're Phasekeeper intelligence," she said.

"Not anymore. The Division fractured. You saw what they made here, didn't you?"

Xinavane didn't answer.

"They thought they could stabilize the Fold. Use those children as anchors. But they lost control." He glanced at the void pulsing behind her. "Now it's eating through layers *they* can't even map."

He took a step closer. "You're connected to one of them, aren't you? The boy."

Xinavane's fingers twitched: a reflex. A thread of invisible force emanated between them.

"You're not walking out of here with that knowledge," she said quietly.

He smirked. "Neither are you."

The hum surged – the walls began bending, light strobing.

The floor buckled.

Xinavane lunged first. Her hands met his forehead, and the psychic ripple hit like electricity through water. His mind snapped open: thoughts, memories, encrypted flashes of classified directives – all flooding through her at once.

And beneath it all, one horrifying truth: The Fold hadn't lost control. It had evolved.

The room convulsed. The void at her back widened, and a pressure wave ripped through the air without sound.

Xinavane snatched her hand away and bolted for the stairwell as the floor dissolved behind her.

Halfway up the steps, she looked back – the agent was gone, swallowed by light.

As she burst through the maintenance door into the emergency wing, she felt it reach her mind again – not Elian, but something else speaking through the Fold's resonance:

He's moving. You can still find him. But the city will fall first.

She stumbled into the hallway, breath ragged. Above her, alarms blared. The hospital lights now flickered violet too.

Atlanta was becoming part of the Fold.

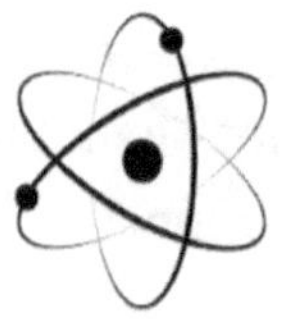

CHAPTER 30

The Safe Zone

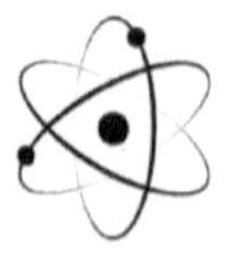

Nyari and Elian reached the edge of downtown just before dawn.

A gutted community center stood there, its entrance lit by a sputtering orange bulb. A sign taped to the glass read:

CITY EMERGENCY RELIEF SITE – AUTHORIZED PERSONNEL ONLY

Voices drifted from inside: low, careful, human.

"Finally," Nyari whispered. "We're not the only ones left."

They slipped through the broken doorway, careful not to crunch the glass beneath their feet.

Inside, cots lined the walls. Plastic tarps divided the space, and the emergency lights painted everything in a dim, reddish glow.

A group of people huddled near a metal barrel fire. Their faces were drawn, pale, eyes darting to Elian and Nyari like animals watching something new enter their territory.

An older woman stepped forward. "You hurt?"

Elian shook his head. "No. Just trying to stay clear of the streets."

The woman nodded slowly. "Then you stay quiet, boy. Whatever's happening out there – it's spreading." She looked toward the covered windows. "They say the air hums now."

Elian and Nyari exchanged a glance. They could both hear it too – beneath everything.

The hum.

It had followed them.

They found a corner away from the others. Nyari scavenged a few protein bars and some old boots for Elian in a supply bin.

"We can rest for a few hours," she said. "Then we move again."

Elian didn't answer. His eyes were fixed on the ceiling. The light fixtures swayed slightly, though there was no wind.

He stood. "Something's wrong."

Nyari sighed. "You haven't slept in thirty-six hours. Everything's wrong."

"No, look."

The lightbulbs stuttered – and for a split second, the entire room shifted. The walls rippled, the cots stretched thin like reflections in water.

The people by the fire didn't seem to notice.

Then, one of them moved twice.

A man turned his head, but his body didn't follow. A lag, like a bad recording.

"Elian…" Nyari whispered.

The hum grew louder.

Across the room, a young woman dropped her cup. It clattered once, twice – then hung in midair, trembling.

She reached for it – and her hand passed through it.

The cup didn't fall. It dissolved.

The room went still.

Then, all at once, the hum erupted: a roar inside their bones. The air twisted, the light fractured like a cracked eggshell into streaks of violet and gold. People screamed. Some vanished mid-run, their outlines scattering into static. Others froze, caught between frames of motion.

"Elian!" Nyari grabbed his arm, dragging him toward the exit. "It's not a safe zone – it's a breach site!"

They ran for the exit, but the hallway ahead warped and split into overlapping versions of itself.

Behind them, voices – layered, distorted, mechanical, all speaking in unison: *Anchor Unstable. Frequency Leaking. Containment Compromised.*

Nyari slammed her palm against the emergency release. The door refused to open.

Elian turned, breath shaking. The light was brighter now, and every surface seemed to breathe. From within the light, figures were forming.

Not agents. Not human.

Shadows of people, made of static – outlines twitching in and out, mouths whispering in reverse.

"Elian!" Nyari shouted. "Do something!"

He reached deep – the instinct he hated, the phasing that had almost killed him before. But now, surrounded by the Fold, it felt different – less like losing control, more like being invited.

The hum synced with his heartbeat.

He stepped forward. The world split.

For a moment, he stood in two realities – one collapsing, one emerging just beneath it. He saw Nyari pulling at the door, the ghosts closing in, the air trembling with every heartbeat.

He reached toward the wall and pushed – not with his hands, but with frequency.

The concrete rippled. Softened.

"Now!" He shouted.

Nyari didn't hesitate. She dove through the wall – vanishing like smoke – and Elian followed, the world snapping shut behind them.

They stumbled into the open air.

Dawn light.

Silence.

They were outside – in the middle of an empty street. The building behind them was gone – erased from the world.

Nyari dropped to her knees, coughing. "What did you just do?"

Elian stared at his hands, still glowing faintly. "I...synced with it."

"With the Fold?"

He nodded. "It's inside everything now."

And for the first time, Elian understood:

They weren't running from the Fold anymore.

They were living inside it.

They both turned toward the skyline. Half of downtown shimmered in and out of existence – like a mirage trying to decide if it should stay.

And Elian and Nyari had to decide where they should go.

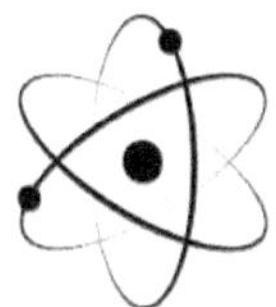 

CHAPTER 31

The Man by the Tracks

They followed the sound of running water until the city fell quiet.

The rain had stopped. Smoke drifted in the air. They walked along what used to be the MARTA rail line, the tracks half-buried beneath moss and debris.

"Elian," Nyari said softly.

"Where are we even going?"

He slowed. "Do you hear that?"

Footsteps.

Someone else was coming down the tracks.

A man appeared through the fog – tall, in a dark coat, moving slowly, one hand raised in cautious greeting. His clothes were soaked, but he didn't slouch as if he were cold or wet.

"Easy," he called. "You don't want to startle me."

Nyari stepped in front of Elian, arm out. "Who are you?"

The man smiled with half his mouth. "Someone who can help. My name is Doctor Doyle. I worked with Dr. Xinavane before she disappeared."

Elian's heart jumped.

"You know her?"

"I did," Doyle said. "She's alive. And she's looking for you."

The words hit like a jolt of electricity.

Nyari narrowed her eyes. "How do we know that's true?"

Doyle didn't flinch. "Because she sent me. She can't move freely – not with the Fold watching everything that emits energy. She needs you two in one place. Somewhere stable enough for her to reach you."

He gestured down the tracks toward a tunnel whose mouth opened wide in the concrete.

"There's a substation beneath Five Points. Shielded walls. The last place they can't trace a frequency through."

Elian hesitated. "The Fold's everywhere. You can't shield from something that's everywhere."

Doyle's smile twitched – almost too quick to notice. "You're right. But we've learned to bend it. She's waiting there. I can take you."

Nyari stepped closer to Elian, voice low. "Something's off."

"I know," he whispered.

Doyle started walking ahead of them, slow and steady. "You'll want to move before the next pulse. The city's about to shift again."

If Doyle was lying, following him could be suicide. If he was telling the truth, it might be the only way to find Xinavane.

They followed.

The tunnel swallowed them in darkness. The air grew warmer, the walls slick with condensation.

Doyle's voice echoed ahead. "You're stronger than she thought, Elian. The Fold responds to you now. It listens."

Elian frowned. "How do you know that?"

Doyle kept walking. "Because *we* built the monitors. The Fold isn't chaos. It's code. It's learning your signal."

Nyari froze. "We?"

Doyle turned then — slow, deliberate.

For the first time, Elian saw his eyes. Not brown. Not even human. Pale silver, like liquid mercury.

"You can't hide from what you are," said Doyle. "You were made for it."

The hum amplified — vibrating through the rails beneath their feet.

Elian staggered back, "You're not working with Xinavane."

"No," Doyle said.

"She's working against her nature. She's working against you."

He reached out.

His outline blurred, then reformed, as if the Fold itself were wearing him as a disguise.

"Run!" Nyari screamed, pulling Elian backward.

The tunnel shuddered – walls flexing inward, cables snapping.

Elian grabbed Nyari's hand and bolted, the sound of the hum chasing them like a living storm.

Behind them, Doyle's voice trailed: *"You can't run from your frequency, Elian. You are the key!"*

They burst into the open night.

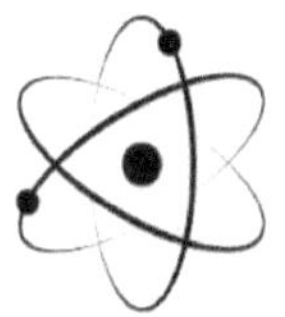

CHAPTER 32

The Reflection

The world had stopped making sense hours ago.

Elian and Nyari scrambled through the wrecked streets, breaths sharp and uneven. Behind them, the tunnel had collapsed. Ahead, cars stood abandoned at odd angles, some half-phased through the pavement.

"Elian...slow down," Nyari gasped, clutching her ribs. "You're bleeding."

He looked down. A thin line of red, visible under the streetlight.

"I'm fine," he said – though it came out more like a tremor than a word.

They ducked down and crawled into the belly of an overturned bus. The air reeked of machine oil and leaking gas.

Outside, the city groaned like something alive.

"Who was that guy?" Nyari whispered. "He said Xinavane sent him."

Elian shook his head. "He wasn't human. Not fully. The Fold was inside him. Like it was wearing him."

"Then, where do we go now?"

He didn't answer. His mind was ringing with Doyle's last words: *You can't run from your frequency.*

Outside, the streetlights went dark — one by one.

Nyari tensed. "What's happening?"

Elian focused on the silence.

A blinding white light flared across the skyline. Windows shattered in the wave. The bus they hid in groaned as the metal twisted — the frame melting like wax.

"Elian!" Nyari screamed, dragging him toward the back exit.

They spilled onto the street as the bus caved in on itself and vanished, leaving only a ripple in the air where it had been.

They ran again.

They turned a corner and found themselves on Edgewood Avenue.

Elian stopped cold.

Through one of the storefronts, he saw something impossible. His hospital room. The bed. IVs. Monitors.

And in the bed – his body.

Nyari grabbed his arm. "Elian, no – don't look."

He took a step forward anyway, transfixed. "It's me."

Then, suddenly, the vision collapsed.

In its place, a cracked mirror lying in the street. And in the mirror's reflection:

The same hospital room.

The same body.

But now, the eyes were open.

"Elian," Nyari whispered, backing away. "We have to move."

The reflection smiled.

Then it stood up.

They sprinted down the street. The crackling sound of distortion chasing them like rolling thunder – buildings and trees bending in unnatural directions as they ran.

They ducked under a bridge to catch their breath.

The world seemed to scream.

Elian squeezed his eyes shut, begging the noise in his head to stop. Behind the static, he felt it again: Xinavane's voice, a ghost of a sound, but it was her:

"Elian. Stay awake. We're coming."

His eyes flew open.

"She's trying to reach me."

Nyari's relief lasted all of two seconds.

Something was moving on the street above them.

Footsteps. Heavy. Synchronized.

Elian pulled Nyari behind a support pillar. Through the cracks, they saw shadow movement. Agents – half-phase suits flickering in and out of sight.

"They've found us," Nyari whispered.

A frantic drumming pulsed in Elian's ears. "Not yet. Not if I can bend first."

He closed his eyes – reaching for the vibration again. The hum inside him matched the one in the air, until both became one sound.

Reality stuttered.

And, in an instant, they both vanished.

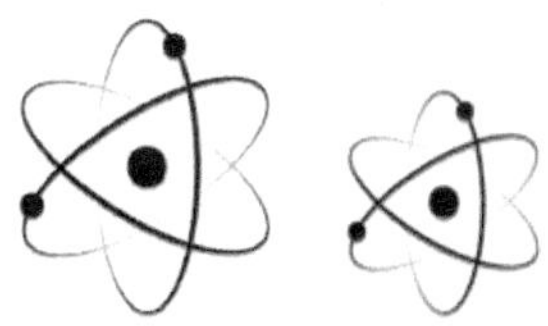

CHAPTER 33

The Signal

A thick fog hung over Atlanta.

From the hospital rooftop, Xinavane watched the skyline sputter and fail like a dying circuit board – whole districts going dark and then blinking back to a sickly glow. The Fold had breached containment and was now streaming through every wire, every cell tower, every pulse of light. She could feel the unseen force beneath her feet. The atmosphere around her felt charged with a current that seeped from the ground and coursed through the city's arteries.

Janelle stood beside her, arms crossed tight. "You're saying the lights are...alive?"

Xinavane didn't look away from the horizon.

"Not alive. Resonant. The Fold's using the city's infrastructure to amplify a signal – his signal."

Marcus leaned on the ledge, staring out at the violet haze crawling along the freeway. "Elian."

"Yes," Xinavane said quietly. "He's bleeding energy into everything. Every time he phases, he sends a shock through reality's framework. It's rewriting the rules."

"Can you stop it?" Janelle's voice cracked, half fear, half fury.

"I can try to reach him, but something is interfering. Our communication has been compromised," Xinavane said. "A dampening field has been built into the grid."

"The agents?"

Xinavane nodded. "They're redirecting his frequency. They want him to fold entirely. If they succeed, the city goes with him."

Marcus turned sharply. "Then what the hell are we still standing here for?"

Xinavane released a jagged breath and pressed her eyes closed. She could sense Elian's energy signature through the noise – erratic, unstable, flaring, and vanishing again.

"He's alive, but he is at his breaking point," she said. "If I reach too hard, I could pull him under."

A single tear landed on Janelle's hand. She wiped at her face. "He doesn't know better...he's just a boy," her lips quivering.

Xinavane opened her eyes. "Not anymore," she said.

"The Fold is adapting to him, learning his rhythm – treating him like a key."

Thunder rolled in the distance, low and metallic.

The skyline flashed silhouettes of downtown's buildings phasing in and out, like reflections in disturbed water.

Marcus stepped back from the ledge. "If the Fold's using him…what is it trying to open?"

Xinavane didn't answer at first, her gaze fixed on a single point downtown – a spinning distortion above Five Points, like a hole punched through the air.

"Something it's been waiting for," she said, finally breaking the silence.

They moved inside the hospital. The halls were empty – power flickering, monitors hissing static. The other patients had been evacuated hours ago.

Xinavane laid out her sensors, blue lights blinking. "These will triangulate his signature," she said. "When he folds, even partially, it leaves a trace in the air."

Marcus paced behind her. "And if the agents are tracking him too?"

"They'll see it," she said. "They just won't understand it."

One of the sensors flared red.

Xinavane froze. "He's close."

Marcus leaned over the table. "How close?"

She adjusted the dials, heart hammering. "Two miles east. Edgewood."

Janelle grabbed her bag. "Then let's go!"

Xinavane hesitated. "Wait…look."

The red signal split in two. One was steady, but dim. The other was flickering, repeating in loops.

Marcus frowned. "What does that mean?"

Xinavane's voice was barely a whisper. "It means they've cloned his resonance. They are trying to make more of him."

The building trembled.

Janelle's knees buckled, and she gripped Marcus's arm. "What's happening?"

Outside, the horizon bent again, the city moving in a slow, impossible motion.

Xinavane stared out the window as the Fold's shimmer crept closer, swallowing blocks at a time. "They've breached containment."

Marcus turned to her. "Then we're out of time."

Xinavane nodded, voice cold, steady. "So, we find him first."

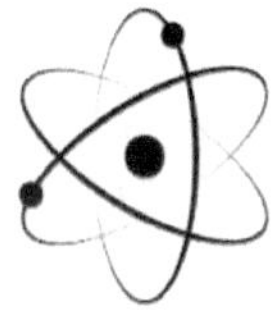

CHAPTER 34

The Mirror City

Elian woke to silence.

Not the kind you hear after a quiet sleep. Not even the kind you hear after an explosion. This was the absence of everything: sound, air, even thought.

Then the hum returned – steady as a heartbeat.

Elian sat up. His palms met cold glass.

He wasn't outside. He wasn't anywhere.

White fog drifted across the surface. Light bent through it, refracting his reflection over and over – hundreds of Elian faces staring back.

"Nyari?" His voice echoed back.

No answer.

He turned slowly. The horizon was endless – a city made of mirrors. Towers rose from the fog, reflecting each other in infinite depth. Every surface shimmered like liquid chrome. There was no sun, but everything glowed faintly, as if lit from the inside.

Elian took a step forward.

His reflection didn't move.

It stood perfectly still, eyes locked on him through the glass. Then it tilted its head.

"You shouldn't have come here."

The voice was his own, layered with static.

"Who are you?" Elian whispered.

The reflection smiled. "I'm what the Fold remembers. I'm what you left behind."

"I didn't mean to –"

"You never mean to," it said, stepping closer. "But you keep touching the edges. You keep letting it in."

Elian backed away, boots squeaking against the glass. "Where's Nyari?"

"She's in the Fold. She's a part of it now."

Elian clenched his fists. "You're lying."

The reflection moved closer, perfectly mirroring him again – until their faces were inches apart through the skin-thin barrier.

"I'm not lying," it said. "I'm becoming."

The voice spoke without static now, perfectly mimicking Elian's.

The world flickered – brief images appearing through the mirror surface:

-The hospital corridor collapsing into light.
-The tunnel warping, like melting plastic.
-Xinavane's face, eyes wide in horror.

Elian staggered back. "What is this place?"

"The Fold," said the reflection. "But not as you knew it. This is the layer between. Where it learns to copy."

"Copy what?"

The reflection laughed. "You...all of you."

A deep vibration shuddered through the air. The mirrored towers around them began to distort and ripple like sound waves.

Elian fell to his knees, looking at the back of his hands. His skin was now the same silver hue as the city.

The reflection knelt too, watching him. "You feel it, don't you? The rhythm. The code."

Elian's pulse matched the hum. His vision blurred – flashes of faces, buildings, light.

"Stop it," he shrieked.

"You can't stop a reflection," it said. "You can only merge."

Then the reflection pressed his palm to the glass. The surface rippled outward, thin as a membrane.

"Come closer," it whispered. "She's waiting on the other side."

"Who?"

The reflection smiled. "Xinavane."

Elian hesitated – the hum grew into a rhythm, finding Elian's heartbeat. The mirrored hand stayed there, inches away. Elian's body moved without consent, drawn by the vibration.

Then –

"Elian. Stop. Don't listen."

Xinavane's voice cut through the static.

The sound snapped him back.

He stumbled away, breaking the rhythm.

The mirror cracked – spiderweb lines racing outward in silence. The reflection's smile vanished. "She can't hold you forever," it hissed. "The Fold remembers its own."

The crack deepened. Light poured through.

Then the world shattered.

Elian hit the ground hard – asphalt beneath him, rain soaking his face. The sky above was violet and trembling. The city's lights pulsed in time with his heartbeat.

Somewhere nearby, sirens wailed.

He rolled on his side in tears.

Nyari was gone. His reflection was gone – but the hum hadn't stopped. It was inside him now.

Lurking.

Waiting.

CHAPTER 35

The Imposter

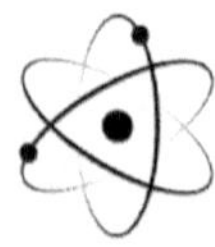

The storm came in sideways.

The skyline vanished behind curtains of rain that seemed to fall both down and up at once. A tide of low curling black clouds rolled over Atlanta like a collapsing ceiling, pierced by wild, unpredictable streaks of lightning, which didn't obey the sky's geometry.

Inside the hospital's command ward, every monitor screamed static.

The grid Xinavane had built from scavenged hardware flickered in rapid succession and patterns she'd never seen before, repeating coordinates that refused to stay still.

Marcus leaned over her shoulder. "Is that him?"

Xinavane stared at the center of the screen. A red light

blinked on the map. Vanished. Reappeared three blocks away.

"It is," she said. "But the frequency is wrong."

Janelle stepped closer. "Wrong how?"

"It's doubled," she said. "His resonance split when he crossed back."

Marcus swore under his breath. "So, you're saying there are two Elian's?"

"No," Xinavane said. "Not two. One, and a reflection that thinks it's him."

Lightning struck and washed the room in violet light. For a split second, a city that wasn't Atlanta reflected in every metal surface – towers of mirrored glass, bent and endless.

Janelle gripped the edge of the table. "Can you tell which one is real?"

Xinavane adjusted the dials. The signals separated into two distinct pulses.

"The true Elian bleeds warmth into the field. The other drains it."

Two points locked onto the map.

-**Edgewood Avenue: weak, unstable.**

-**Decatur Street: bright, steady, cold.**

Marcus pointed. "Decatur's stronger. That's where we go."

Xinavane shook her head. "That's the echo. It's feeding on the city's grid. The Fold wants us to see it."

"So, where's Elian?" Janelle demanded.

"Edgewood," Xinavane said. "Barely holding together."

Thunder shook the windows, rattling the glass. The lights cut out – just darkness and the rhythm of machines still running without power.

Marcus checked his pistol, even though they all knew bullets meant nothing against the Fold. "We split up," he said, already reaching for his jacket. "I'll take Decatur. Draw it away if I can.

Janelle started to argue.

"You're with me," Xinavane said firmly. "We get the real one."

Xinavane packed the last transmitter into her coat and paused at the door.

Beneath the thunder, Xinavane felt something else.

A shift.

"Elian just woke up," she said softly.

Marcus frowned. "That's good, right?"

Xinavane shook her head. "Not if the other one did too."

They stepped outside. The city's rain had turned on itself, falling upward into the clouds.

Janelle looked up. "The sky is broken."

Xinavane didn't look up. She was already scanning the street. Her handheld sensor pulsed red – then split.

Two signals.

Moving.

Toward each other.

She lowered the device, her throat dry.

"He's not alone anymore," she whispered. "The echo is hunting him."

Lightning cracked across the sky, bathing the city in molten silver.

Somewhere in that glow, two identical signatures – beating in perfect sync, were closing the distance, as if the world itself were trying to stitch the same soul back into one body.

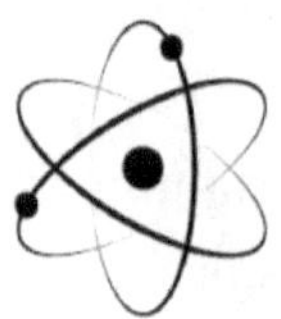

CHAPTER 36

Haunted

The rain hissed against the streetlights.

Elian moved fast – hood up, breath sharp in the cold. His hospital gown was gone now, replaced by scavenged clothes from a laundromat bin: jeans too big, a hoodie that smelled faintly of smoke.

He didn't remember how long he'd been walking. Just that he couldn't stop. Every time he slowed down, something caught up.

He saw it first in reflections – the ones that didn't behave. Storefront windows lagged, showing his silhouette a beat too late. Once, in the dark chrome of a parked car, his reflection looked back up at him.

Not at him. Through him.

Elian stumbled back, nearly slipping on the wet pavement. The image in the metal *didn't* fall. It just tilted its head, curious.

"No," he whispered. "You're not real."

The reflection smiled – his smile, only slower.

He ran.

Ran until his lungs burned, until the sound of traffic faded and the streets grew quiet. Somewhere in the distance, a siren wailed – then cut off mid-note.

He ducked into an alley near Edgewood, squeezing between dumpsters. His hands shook as he pressed the abandoned cell phone to his chest. No signal.

"Xinavane," he whispered. "Please find me."

A drip echoed.

Then another.

He froze.

The puddle by his boot rippled – not from the rain, but from something beneath the surface.

The reflection in the water wasn't the alley at all.

It was...another place. A street he remembered, but wrong. Everything moved backwards. People walking in reverse. Rain climbing back into the clouds. And standing there, clear as breath on glass, was him.

Same face. Same torn hoodie.

But its eyes, the eyes glowed silver.

Elian swallowed hard. "What are you?"

"I'm you," the reflection said.

The voice came from behind him.

Elian spun — nothing there.

The puddle bulged upward like liquid skin.

He ran out of the alley — across the street, weaving through shadows. Every window caught his image and held it — like a trail of living ghosts marking his path.

He didn't dare look back, but he could feel it gaining.

He ran frantically down a side street until he reached an old train tunnel, his vision was splitting — real and reflection, the city and the overlapping Fold, flickering in and out of sync.

His face followed him everywhere now — in puddles, in glass, even in the faint sheen of his own skin.

He dropped to his knees, pressing his palms to the cold concrete.

"Stop," he ordered. "You're not me."

The air behind him rippled.

"Then who are you?"

He spun around — nothing but a shimmer, like steam rising from asphalt.

Then, for one terrible second, his own outline peeled away from the heat and smiled – cold and menacing.

Then it was gone.

Elian shuffled backward as the tunnel swallowed him in darkness.

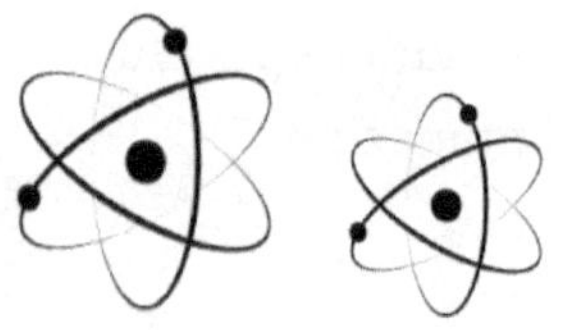

CHAPTER 37

Search and Rescue

Miles away, in the back of a black SUV, a scanner pinged.

Two identical signals. Both active. Both moving toward convergence.

The rain had turned metallic by the time they hit Edgewood. Each droplet shimmered for a fraction of a second before vanishing midair, leaving trails of static that crawled across the windshield.

Xinavane drove with one hand on the wheel, the other gripping the frequency scanner. The red pulse blinked erratically – sometimes near, sometimes miles away, never steady.

Beside her, Janelle clutched the dashboard. "It's jumping again."

"I know." Xinavane's voice was tight. "He's moving too

fast...or something's copying his pattern."

"You mean –"

"Yes." She didn't finish the sentence. The Fold didn't need names. It only needs familiarity.

The scanner chimed – twice.

One bright. One dim. Elian and his reflection.

Xinavane studied the screen. "He's close. Less than half a mile."

Janelle leaned forward. "Which one?"

"That's the question."

She turned down a side street and slowed. The SUV rolled to a stop near the mouth of an old train tunnel. The scanner's pulses were almost overlapping now – two heartbeats trying to occupy the same rhythm.

Xinavane killed the engine. The sudden hush felt louder than actual sound.

Janelle stared out the window. "Marcus said he'd sweep Decatur Street," she said, breaking the silence. "If he's not answering, maybe he – "

"Don't," Xinavane cut in. "We focus on Elian."

The scanner stabilized. Both signals were inside the tunnel.

"Together?" Janelle asked.

"Not yet," Xinavane said. "But they're close. And if they merge…"

She didn't finish.

They stepped out into the storm. The rain felt heavier here. Every few seconds, the streetlights glitched between warm yellow, and the Fold's cold violet.

Xinavane adjusted the small black device strapped to her wrist. The air around it shimmered, forming a field that distorted the reflections near her.

"Stay inside the dampening field," she said. "If the echo senses you, it'll use your mind to find him faster."

Janelle got into position near Xinavane.

"Keep your eyes off mirrors," Xinavane added. "And if you hear your son's voice somewhere it shouldn't be – don't answer."

They descended into the tunnel. Water dripped steadily from the concrete ceiling.

Halfway down, the scanner chimed again. The stronger signal was moving slowly, as if it were searching. The weaker one trembled, barely holding form.

Xinavane felt it in her chest before she saw it. "He's trying to hide."

"From what?" Janelle asked.

"From himself."

A vibration rolled beneath the tracks, but no train was coming. The tunnel lights flickered. One by one, they changed colors until they burned a deep, unnatural blue.

Janelle froze. "What *is* that?"

Xinavane's hand found her arm. "They're converging. Were out of time."

She raised the dampening device and stepped forward. The air wavered like gas fumes.

And through it, she saw him.

Elian. Kneeling near the far wall, his outline jumping between two forms. One flesh. One made of light.

The echo was almost complete.

Xinavane's pulse spiked. She felt the hum in her skull – the Fold recognizing her.

She shouted across the tunnel: "Elian, don't look at it!"

He turned away.

And the tunnel exploded with light. The two frequencies drifted out of alignment.

When the glare faded, Janelle was on the ground, coughing.

Xinavane stood over her, eyes wide.

The scanner was dead – melted from the inside out.

Janelle's eyes searched the tunnel. "Elian," Janelle whispered.

But there was no answer.

Only a faint, overlapping echo – like two heartbeats fading into one.

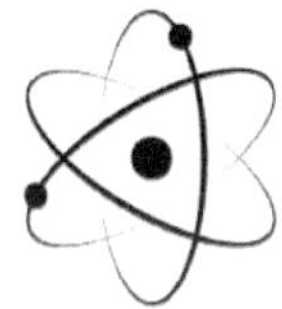 

CHAPTER 38

The One Who Remained

At first, there was only ringing.

A single endless tone in Xinavane's skull that swallowed every other sound.

When she opened her eyes, the tunnel had changed. Its walls were blurry behind thin membranes of light – like heat above desert sand.

She sat up slowly. Her clothes were soaked. Her scanner lay beside her, split open, smoke curling from its circuits.

"Janelle?"

A weak cough answered.

Xinavane turned. Janelle was slumped against the wall, hands slick with something dark. Not blood – but something that glowed violet in the dim light.

"Are you hurt?"

Janelle blinked hard, disoriented. "Where is he?"

Xinavane looked down the tunnel.

Elian stood there.

He was standing perfectly still in a wash of blue light, head lowered, breathing too slowly. His shadow stretched in two directions, as if the light couldn't decide which way to fall.

"Stay here," Xinavane said.

Janelle's voice was hoarse. "Is it him?"

"I don't know."

The ground buzzed beneath Xinavane's boots as she approached. Each step made the air shiver. The closer she got, the colder it felt.

"Elian," she said softly. "Can you hear me?"

No answer.

She reached out, hesitated, then placed her hand gently on his shoulder.

The fabric of his hoodie was damp beneath her fingers, yet it was warm to the touch – solid in a way that felt like proof.

Relief fluttered in her chest.

Then he looked up.

His eyes caught the light wrong. One flashed metallic gray.

Xinavane's skin prickled with goosebumps. "Elian," she whispered again. "Do you know where you are?"

He blinked. Slow, mechanical.

Then he spoke – and it was his voice. But the voice had the precision of machinery, each word perfect *and* wrong at the same time.

"I...made it out," he said.

Behind her, Janelle sobbed. "Oh my God – Elian!"

She rushed forward and wrapped her arms around him. For a moment, he stood there – stiff, uncertain. Then his hands lifted and rested lightly on her back.

Janelle pulled away, cupping his face. "Baby, look at me."

He smiled.

It was perfect. Rehearsed.

"Mom."

The single word sent a shiver down Xinavane's spine. Not because it was wrong. But because it sounded learned – like someone had taught it how to sound right.

The tunnel lights flickered.

Every wet surface became a mirror – and for an instant, Xinavane could see two silhouettes standing where Elian was. One solid, one made of silver static.

Then the tunnel lights stabilized.

Only one shadow remained.

"Elian," Xinavane said carefully. "Tell me what happened before we found you."

He blinked. "I ran."

"And after?"

He hesitated. "After?"

"Yes."

A pause. The walls whispered.

Elian tilted his head slightly – the same motion she'd seen in the reflections. "I woke up here."

Janelle pressed her hand to his cheek. "He's scared – can't you see that?"

Xinavane didn't look away from his eyes. "He's something," she murmured.

Behind them, the broken scanner beeped once.

A weak pulse of red light.

For a heartbeat, two signals flashed again on its ruined display.

Then one winked out.

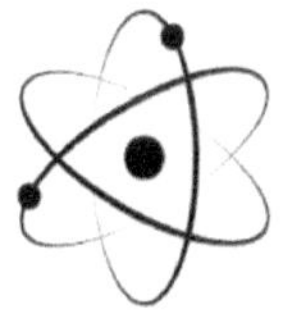

CHAPTER 39

The Memory Test

The storm had passed, but the winds lingered behind.

The tunnel inhaled and exhaled, dragging cold air across its walls. Every few seconds, the ground tremored, as if something deep below was shifting in its sleep.

They'd built a small fire from broken pallets and hospital gauze. Its smoke curled upward and vanished into the dark. The light barely reached ten feet. Beyond that, the shadows looked thick enough to touch.

Elian sat beside the flame, knees drawn up to his chest. His hoodie steamed faintly as it dried. He hadn't spoken in nearly an hour.

Janelle stayed close, brushing his hair off his forehead, the way only a mother could. "You're freezing," she whispered.

He didn't answer. Just stared into the fire, eyes like twin mirrors catching every flicker.

Xinavane sat across from him, elbows on her knees, watching carefully.

Something in his stillness felt wrong. Too quiet. Too composed. As if he were listening to something no one else could hear.

"Elian," she said softly. "Do you remember what you told me the first night in the ward?"

His gaze shifted, slow, gradual. "Which night?"

"The one after the second surgery. When you woke up crying."

He blinked once. "I said...it hurt."

"That's right," Xinavane nodded. But you said something else, too."

Janelle looked up. "Xinavane, what are you doing?"

Xinavane didn't answer. Her focus didn't leave the boy. "Elian – do you remember what you saw in your dream that night?"

He frowned slightly, like he was searching through a file instead of a memory. "A ceiling fan?"

"And?"

He hesitated. "And...a voice. Yours."

"What did I say?"

"You said…" His lips parted, then closed again. A vein of light crawled across his cheek, gone as quickly as it appeared. "You…you didn't want me to be afraid."

Xinavane's throat tightened. "That's not what I said."

Janelle's voice sharpened. "Xinavane –"

"I asked what you heard," Xinavane continued, "not what you felt."

Janelle stood. "Enough! He's exhausted –"

Xinavane's tone softened, almost gentle. "Tell me about the Fold, Elian. What does it feel like?"

He looked up slowly. "Warm."

"Warm?"

"Yes," he smiled. "Like home."

The sound of dripping water stopped.

The fire dimmed.

Xinavane's heart rate elevated instantly. "You never called it that before," she said.

He tilted his head again – the motion slow and mechanical. "You never asked me the right way until now."

Janelle took a step back, fear creeping into her voice. "What…what are you saying?"

Elian's expression softened. "I'm saying you found me. Isn't that what you wanted?"

He looked at her like a reflection trying to remember warmth – his eyes were kind, but empty where it mattered most.

"I came back for you," he said.

And then, a sound echoed from the far end of the tunnel. Footsteps in water.

Xinavane rose slowly. "Stay behind me."

Elian didn't move.

Janelle's voice shook. "Is it…him?"

Xinavane didn't look away. "He's safe…for now."

 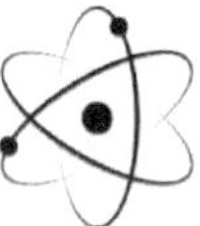

CHAPTER 40

The New Arrival

Xinavane took a step towards the tunnel's mouth, hands raised, palms turned slightly outward.

"Janelle," she whispered, "Move behind the fire."

Janelle didn't move. She was staring at Elian – or the boy that looked like him, still seated by the orange glow.

"Elian," Xinavane said carefully. "Stand up."

He did. Too smoothly, like a puppet lifting on invisible strings.

Another figure moved toward them, half-seen through the smoke of the fire.

"Who's there?" Janelle called out.

The new arrival moved into view – clothes torn, lip split, eyes wide and wild with fear.

It was Elian.

The real one.

He froze when he saw them — saw himself standing by the fire. "Don't — don't go near it!" he screamed. "That's not me!"

The other Elian turned slowly and steadily. The corners of his mouth curled up, and his eyes — where irises should have been — were lit with shifting blue lines.

Janelle let out a sound that was half sob, half disbelief. "No, no —"

Xinavane didn't hesitate; she stepped between them, her hand flaring with vibration, and then — a spark in the dark. Static discharge, creating tiny arcs of light, could be seen against her skin, like miniature lightning. "Stay back, both of you."

The false Elian smiled wider. "Why are you fighting this?" His voice echoed. "You wanted him safe. He's safe with us."

"You're not him. You're a resonance. A bleed." Xinavane's voice barely rose above a breath, but the words held weight.

"Maybe," it replied, looking back to Elian. "Or, maybe I'm the part that learned to live without him."

It reached a hand toward the real Elian, who flinched and clutched at his chest as if something were being pulled outward.

Xinavane reacted instantly, thrusting both palms forward.

The air cracked – not like thunder, but like glass splitting underwater.

The false Elian's image scattered into threads of light, each strand whipping upward, twisting toward the ceiling, and vanishing like smoke sucked through an invisible seam.

The tunnel fell silent.

Elian collapsed to his knees, gasping. Janelle caught him and pulled him into her arms, sobbing against his shoulder.

Xinavane stayed still, listening – but beneath the quiet, she could still feel it.

The Fold remained anchored to the horizon.

Still active.

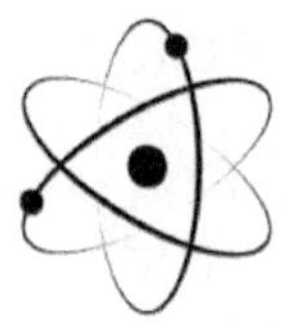

CHAPTER 41

The City Trembles

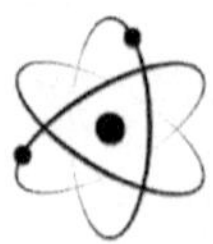

Marcus drove with one hand locked around the steering wheel, eyes darting up and down the streets, scanning every shadow.

Every block felt stranger than the last.

And somewhere in the distance, a woman could be heard crying. Her screams tore from her throat, raw, ugly, as if the sound were being yanked from her chest.

He slowed at an intersection where a crowd had gathered — people standing perfectly still, heads tilted slightly upward, eyes unfocused.

The winds shifted.

And beneath it, he heard something else — like a child singing through a wall. It was coming from under the old underpass.

Spikes of electromagnetic noise rose and fell like ocean tides around him. Every time the frequency peaked, his chest burned. The closer he drove, the stronger the pulse.

At the underpass, he killed the engine and stepped out. His shoes sank into the shallow puddles with a splash.

A shape moved in the dark.

"Xinavane?" he called.

His voice lingered unnaturally, overstaying its echo, stretching past where sound should have died.

A figure stepped from the shadows.

"Marcus?"

Xinavane's face was drawn and exhausted, but her eyes still held that dangerous calm. Janelle followed close behind, clutching Elian's hand – the real one this time – though the boy looked barely conscious, swaying weakly with every step.

Marcus rushed to them. "You're alive."

"Barely," Xinavane said, glancing back into the tunnel. The fire was gone, but the air still smelled scorched.

"It tried to pull him back. It sent a copy first – a decoy."

Marcus crouched in front of Elian. "What happened?"

Elian's eyes fluttered open. For an instant, faint blue lines spidered across his skin — then vanished.

"It wasn't just pretending," Elian whispered. "It was learning."

Janelle wrapped her arms around him. "Don't talk, just breathe, baby."

But Xinavane's gaze had gone distant, listening. The hum was spreading now – flowing through the streets, through the buildings, through the city itself.

Somewhere far above, a low metallic groan swept across the skyline.

They all froze.

A transformer exploded in the distance – blue light flaring, then darkness swallowing half the block.

Marcus looked up. "What does that mean?"

"It means," Xinavane said quietly, "the Fold has found its frequency."

Elian stirred in Janelle's arms. "It's not gone," he murmured. "It's in everything now. The glass. The light. The air."

The streetlight above them flickered once – twice – and for a moment, their reflections on the wet pavement didn't move when they did.

Marcus took a slow breath. "Then we move. Now. Somewhere off the grid."

Xinavane nodded. "Atlanta won't hold," she said. "The resonance will track him through the circuitry. We need grounding – something old. Something untouched."

"Like what?"

Her eyes shifted east.

"Stone Mountain."

Marcus glanced back toward the tunnel – where just for a second, a child's silhouette shimmered at the edge of the dark. Not moving. Just watching.

When he blinked, it was gone.

The wind brushed cold across his neck.

And for the first time, Marcus realized that the hum was alive and was searching for them.

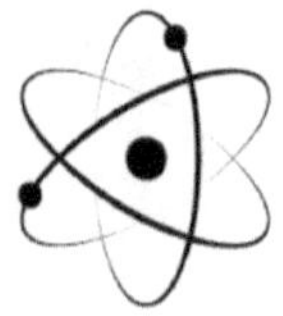

CHAPTER 42

The Static Road

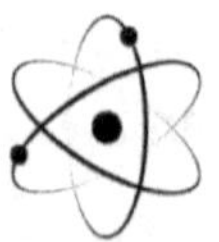

Marcus gunned the van through broken streets, glass crunching beneath the tires, as the skyline flickered behind them in spasms of dying light. The power grid was collapsing. Whole blocks plunged into darkness, then flared back alive in colors that didn't belong to this world.

Xinavane sat rigid in the passenger seat, one hand braced on the dash, the other pressed to her temple. She was listening again.

In the backseat, Elian stirred. A pale glow beneath his closed eyelids, seeping through his skin.

Marcus kept one eye on the rearview mirror. "How far to Stone Mountain?"

"Seventeen miles," Xinavane said. "If the road still exists."

They tore through the edge of Atlanta like a skipped heartbeat – one moment deep in the city, the next in a half-lit
maze of highways that no longer matched the map. Every
sign they passed repeated itself: *EXIT 41…EXIT 41…EXIT 41.*

Janelle gripped Elian's shoulders. "Stay with me, baby."

"They're still calling me," his voice small. "They don't know
which one I am."

Marcus clenched the wheel, eyes shifting between his boy
and the road. "Well, ignore them all. We're getting you out
of here."

The road curved east – and for a moment, the world
stretched. The van's reflection lagged, delayed by a fraction
of a second. Then it snapped back, the steering wheel kick-
ing in Marcus's hand. He swore under his breath, steadying
them.

Ahead, something burned.

A transport van lay overturned and smoking – identical to
the one that had taken Elian.

Marcus slowed.

Xinavane whispered, "Don't stop."

Too late.

The road warped, asphalt bleeding into shadow. From the
wreckage, figures limped out – agents, or what was left of
them. Their limbs twitched at freakish angles, their bodies
stuttering like corrupted video frames. One raised a gun,

but the weapon flickered and dissolved into static.

"Go!" Xinavane shouted.

Marcus floored it. The van roared ahead just as one of the agents phased straight through the windshield.

Janelle screamed.

The man's face blurred inches from Marcus's. His voice layered like two people speaking at once. "He belongs to us."

Elian shot upright, his eyes blazing with pure static. A burst of white light exploded from the back seat. The agent was hurled through the roof like smoke sucked into a vent.

The van's engine coughed, sparks spilling across the dashboard.

Then — nothing.

Only the hum of the Fold filling the air.

Marcus tried the ignition again. Dead. Every display flickered with nonsense: spirals, numbers repeating — his own reflection wasn't moving with him.

"We walk," Xinavane said.

They stepped into a haunted roadway. Ghost traffic streamed past — cars without drivers, headlights floating through other layers of time.

Elian stumbled. His shadow split in two.

Janelle caught him. "What's happening to him?"

"The Fold feeds on reflection, but the mountain doesn't carry one," Xinavane said. "The closer we get, the thinner the boundary becomes."

They moved on, as Atlanta dimmed behind them. Street-lights leaned like dying trees. Marcus looked back and saw the city flicker like a broken reel of film, burning and reform-ing. Skyscrapers fading into nothing.

Only Stone Mountain stayed still on the horizon.

By the time they reached the forest line, dawn was strug-gling to rise. The air vibrated with a deep, bone-shaking fre-quency.

Elian collapsed to his knees.

"It's awake."

Xinavane froze. "What is?"

Elian pointed toward the dark silhouette of the mountain. Beneath the granite, something stirred – too regularly to be geological. Each pulse rattled the leaves around them.

Marcus backed away in disbelief. "That's not possible."

Xinavane closed her eyes as the hum rose. "It's not the Fold," she whispered. "It's what's keeping it out."

The ground trembled. A surge of static rolled through the trees, bending them toward the mountain like iron to a magnet.

The group fell to the earth as the sound swelled – low, an-cient, alive.

They had reached the edge of the Fold.

And the mountain was waiting.

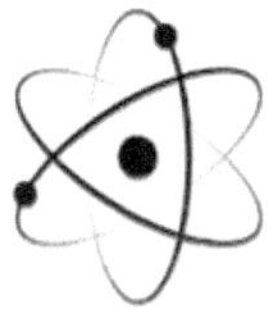

CHAPTER 43

The Living Stone

When the shaking stopped, the silence that followed was unsettling, as though the world was bracing for something else.

Marcus rose slowly, scanning the trees. The forest around Stone Mountain had gone entirely still. Even the insects seemed to have fallen quiet.

The calm before the storm.

Xinavane stood at the edge of the clearing, eyes closed, palms pressed to the soil. Damp locs clung to her face. Her voice was barely audible. "It's awake, but not hostile. Not yet."

Janelle knelt beside Elian, who sat trembling like a plucked string.

"He can feel it," Xinavane murmured. "The Fold is closing in. The mountain is pushing back."

Marcus crouched beside them. "Pushing back? It's rock."

Xinavane opened her eyes, and for a moment, Marcus saw something layered inside them – reflection upon reflection, like mirrors facing each other.

"Stone has frequency," she said. "Granite, especially. It remembers pressure, heat, weight, time. This mountain has been resonating for millions of years. It's the only thing the Fold can't mimic."

Elian shuddered. "It's calling me."

"No," Xinavane's voice sharpened. "It's warning you."

A gust of wind tore through the trees, carrying the scent of rain and iron. The clouds churned overhead, flashes of blue lightning lacing their underbelly. The Fold wasn't far – the horizon was unsteady.

Marcus pointed. "We need higher ground. If we stay in the clearing, were exposed."

Xinavane nodded. "Then we climb."

They began the ascent.

The trail up Stone Mountain was broken and uneven – paths splitting, reforming, leading them in loops that shouldn't exist.

Marcus left marks on the stone with a rusty tire iron, but when they passed the same spot minutes later, the marks were gone.

Elian kept stopping, pressing his ear to the rock.

"I can hear voices inside," he whispered.

"The other boy?" Janelle asked.

He shook his head. "Us. But…later."

Marcus felt a cold weight crawl up his spine. "Xinavane, what the hell does that mean?"

"It means the Fold is already bending time."

They pushed on, breath short in the thick, humid air. The hum grew stronger – not a noise, but a vibration in the ribs. The closer they came to the summit, the more their shadows peeled away from their bodies, clinging to the rock like reluctant ghosts.

When the tree line finally broke, the mountain's bald granite face appeared before them – gray and vast under a swirling sky. Lightning flashed, briefly illuminating the carved figures on the monument, before hurling them back into darkness.

At the base of the carvings, the rock was split – a narrow opening, like a wound running deep into the stone.

Elian stopped and pointed. "That's where it's coming from," he said.

Xinavane knelt before the opening. She could feel the pulse radiating from it – slow and powerful.

"The Fold didn't create this crack in the stone, but it can flow through a weakness that is already exposed. The mountain isn't perfectly sealed, and the Fold only needs the tiniest opening to spill into the physical world."

She reached toward it.

"Xinavane!" Marcus shouted.

Too late.

The vibration surged through her body – and in that instant, she saw. Not with her eyes, but with the resonance frequency that connected every mind the Fold had ever touched.

She saw Atlanta layered in hundreds of versions – burned, drowned, frozen, flickering – stacked like translucent photographs, each one showing a different time and place. And beneath them all, the Fold trying to compress every possibility into one single, obedient pattern.

But through it all, Stone Mountain thundered with a countersignal, a pure frequency holding the line, refusing to yield.

Xinavane gasped, jerking her hand back. Light raced through her veins, then faded just as fast.

"This mountain anchors reality and resists the Fold's distortion," she said. "This place still carries the world's original frequency."

Elian stepped closer to the widening crack. "Then it's the only thing that can save me."

"Wait – "

Janelle reached for him, but the ground shuddered beneath them.

A low roar came from the hole: shredded distortion, as if the sound itself were being fed through a meat grinder.

Marcus dragged Janelle back. The air filled with static. Leaves spun in upward spirals.

Xinavane turned to Elian, eyes wide, pupils trembling, as if already mourning. "If you do this, you won't come back the same version of yourself," fear finally cracking her composure.

Elian met her gaze, surprisingly calm. "Maybe losing a part of me is better than losing all of you."

Cold light poured from the mountain, flooding the summit. For a moment, everything stood still – the world caught in the pause before something breaks.

And then, from within the light, the Fold let out a scream.

CHAPTER 44

The Crossing

Wind slammed across the summit.

The gash in the granite throbbed brighter now, its edges flowing like liquid glass trying to form a mouth. With every surge of light, reality buckled: trees folding inward, the distant sky blinking between day and night.

Marcus pulled Janelle back, shielding his eyes. "What's happening?"

Xinavane didn't answer; she was staring at Elian, who stood a few feet from the opening now, hair lifting in the static, his image ghosting in and out of sight.

"Elian," she said softly, stepping closer. "You don't have to do this alone."

He turned, eyes filled with a storm of static. "I already am."

Then the ground split wider – with a dreadful sound, like

thunder. The Fold poured through – a living storm of color and sound, faces forming and dissolving in endless waves, each one whispering his name.

Xinavane reached out, desperate to close the last inches, but the air bent between them, hardening like glass against her touch, keeping her out.

"Elian!"

He looked over his shoulder, calm amid the chaos. "I can hear them all. Every version of me that didn't make it. Every world that failed."

"Then let me help you stay grounded," she pleaded. "Before you lose your footing – before you slip away...please!"

Another voice cut through the static: impossibly familiar.

"Elian."

He stopped cold.

"Nyari?"

Her figure appeared beside him – translucent, like light struggling through deep water. She looked just as she had that night in the alley – scraped hands, fearless smile, eyes full of defiance. "You still don't see who you are to this place," she said. "This was never about escape. It was about choosing who you become."

He reached for her, but his hand passed through light. "They took you –"

"No," she said gently. "They took one version of me. I'm still here. In the Fold. In the spaces between."

The wind howled in layered tones. The mountain quaked.

Nyari drifted closer, her radiance thinning at the edge of her form. "Elian, don't try to outrun it, force it to recalibrate around you."

He stared at her, the meaning sinking in.

Janelle screamed his name. Marcus tried to run forward, but the Fold's pressure drove them back.

Elian's feet lifted from the stone. He looked at Janelle and Marcus, then at the hole in the mountain yawning before him. The light inside was blinding now, showing glimpses of cities folded in infinite recursion – every version of Atlanta imploding, reassembling, dissolving again.

Tears filled his eyes. He looked at Nyari. "Will you stay with me?"

She smiled. "Always."

He drew a deep breath, and then he drifted into the light.

The sound that followed was not an explosion – it was everything at once, collapsing into a single tone. The hole flared outward, swallowing sky and stone in blinding radiance. Xinavane threw her arms over her face as the shockwave hurled them to the ground.

For a heartbeat, all of them saw through him – Elian, illuminated, in the center of the light, his form breaking apart. Nyari beside him, her hand in his, both dissolving into the wave.

Xinavane's mind filled with resonance, revealing patterns beyond language: ancient and newborn – exposing the Fold rewriting itself around human thought.

Then, suddenly, a snap – like pressure releasing.

Light vanished.

The mountain was still again.

The crack was sealed.

Marcus rose slowly, helping Janelle to her feet. "He's gone," she whispered.

Xinavane knelt where the fissure had been, palms flat on the stone. The granite was warm, vibrating faintly beneath her touch.

"No," she said softly. "He's not gone."

Janelle wiped her eyes. "How can you be sure?"

Xinavane leaned her forehead against the rock – the hum deepened beneath her touch. "He's still phasing. He is using his ability to bend space, to bend the Fold from within."

Wind swept across the summit, and for a moment, they all heard it – a faint, harmonic note that might have been laughter.

Then the sound faded, leaving only the whisper in the trees, and the hum of the living stone.

And somewhere inside the resonance, Nyari and Elian

moved together – no longer haunted, no longer lost, part of a frequency that would never fade.

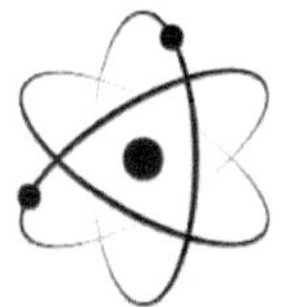

EPILOGUE

The New Signal

Atlanta pretended to move on after Stone Mountain. The city looked the same – traffic lights blinking, MARTA buses sighing down cracked streets.

People chalked up the strange days to solar flares, bad infrastructure, or summer storms. They ignored the clocks drifting out of sync, the dogs barking at empty intersections.

They ignored the children.

On a quiet street near East Lake station, twelve-year-old Horace Meridian stood at the crosswalk, watching the traffic light freeze mid-blink, not change – but freeze. Cars paused in place mid-motion, their tires suspended a hair above the asphalt.

Except, Horace could move inside of it.

He stepped forward, listening to a new sound that had started in his chest a week earlier – a soft internal ticking, like a clock, but not a clock made of gears; it was something...stranger. A biological mechanism that had awakened after the Stone Mountain event. A regulator. A pulse that let him slip between seconds instead of being carried by them.

The breeze halted, and the leaves stopped mid-fall. Horace reached out and touched the frozen air. The moment cracked like thin ice.

Time shuddered. Restarted. Cars lurched through the intersection. Pedestrians blinked, confused.

Horace exhaled shakily. He didn't know why he could do this.

Only that the ticking grew louder every day.

And that something in the world was calling to him.

Across the city, in Grant Park, a thirteen-year-old girl named Eshe Amara knelt beside the small, still body of her dog in the wet grass, under the pecan tree.

She pressed her forehead to the dog's fur, sobbing until her breath shook dust from the ground. Her tears fell – clear, then glowing – coalescing into gold powder as they struck the leaves. When the tears hit the dog's chest, the gold dust sank through his fur and skin, like light through water.

The earth hummed.

The dog inhaled. Not gently, violently – like something yanked its soul back from a boundary it had already crossed.

Eshe gasped and clutched the animal against her.

Eshe didn't notice the way the grass bent toward her.

Behind her, the pecan tree blossomed out of season.

On the rooftop of a rundown Memorial Drive motel, Dr. Xinavane Medousa lifted her head, one palm pressed to the concrete. Her breath caught in her chest.

She felt it all.

Elian's presence buried in the Fold. Nyari being rewritten by the Fold. Horace freezing time without meaning to. Eshe resurrecting the dead with golden tears.

Three forces. Space. Time. Life. Aligned enough to form a pattern she could almost see.

"This isn't random," she thought. "The Fold is waking up because of these children."

Marcus stepped onto the rooftop behind her, boots crunching in the gravel, jacket half-zipped, eyes raw from sleeplessness.

"Tell me you felt that?"

Xinavane didn't answer at first. Her pupils had dilated into deep black pools, reflecting the city's lights below. She craned her neck as if listening to a voice only she could hear.

"It's stronger than before," she said finally. "Something inside the Fold is pushing back."

"Is it him?" Marcus asked, voice cracking on the words.

"Partly," her jaw tightened. "But there's another source. A second frequency."

Marcus grimaced. "Another kid?"

"Not a kid," Xinavane pushed back from the ledge. "A disturbance."

The air shifted. Marcus felt it again: A pressure against his temples, like a headache from somewhere outside his skull. A ripple silently swept across the skyline.

Traffic lights winked out, then flared back to life.

A bird spiraled out of the sky and crashed into the motel roof at their feet.

Dead.

Marcus took a step back. "Tell me that's not connected."

Xinavane knelt beside the fallen bird. It was still warm. She pressed two fingers to its tiny skull.

"Something or someone is destabilizing the boundary," she said.

As if answering her, a deep **BOOM** rolled across the city — too soft to be thunder, too distant to be an explosion. The motel's metal railing vibrated. Below them, dogs began howling, and alarms began to trip one by one: car sirens, store security systems, a chorus of shrill cries. People stepped out onto their balconies in their pajamas, staring upward, confused and uneasy.

Marcus grabbed the railing. "That wasn't normal."

"No," Xinavane said softly. "It was a warning."

Lights across downtown flared white, and then died all at once – plunging Atlanta into a sudden, unnatural darkness.

Marcus grabbed Xinavane's arm. "We have to go. Right now."

But Xinavane couldn't move. She was staring eastward, toward the thick dark, beyond the skyline. Something was opening there.

Not a crack.

Not a portal.

A shadow – swallowing the night, giving it shape.

Marcus followed her gaze.

"What's that?"

"The Fold is waking up," Xinavane said.

And as the shadow widened, something stepped through.

Human-sized.

Human-shaped.

But not human.

Its body rippling like ink suspended in water. The figure lifted its head, scanning the perimeter.

Marcus stumbled back, "Tell me that's not coming for us."

"It's not," her voice low. "It's coming for the children."

And from somewhere deep inside the Fold — quiet but unmistakable —

Elian screamed.

THE END

About the Author

Abner Al-Ameen is a storyteller drawn to the space between reality and the unknown — where the mind, memory, and unseen forces collide.

His debut novel, In Between Worlds: The Passage of Elian, explores what happens when a child's subconscious becomes a doorway... and something on the other side begins to answer back.

Blending psychological tension with surreal science fiction, Abner writes stories that ask a simple but unsettling question:

What if reality isn't as solid as we believe?

Based in Atlanta, Georgia, he continues to build a universe where the impossible isn't just possible — it's watching.

This is only the beginning.

Connect with Abner:

On TikTok: @inbetweenworldsbook

Or Gmail: inbetweenworldsbook@gmail.com

Follow for updates, behind-the-scenes content, and upcoming releases in the In Between Worlds series.